# DR TALL, DARK...AND DANGEROUS?

BY
LYNNE MARSHALL

MILLS & BOON

First published in Great Britain 2012
by Mills & Boon, an imprint of Harlequin (UK) Limited.
Harlequin (UK) Limited, Eton House,
18-24 Paradise Road, Richmond, Surrey TW9 1SR

© Janet Maarschalk 2012

ISBN: 978 0 263 89185 0

Harlequin (UK) policy is to use papers that are natural, renewable and recyclable products and made from wood grown in sustainable forests. The logging and manufacturing process conform to the legal environmental regulations of the country of origin.

Printed and bound in Spain
by Blackprint CPI, Barcelona

**Lynne Marshall** has been a Registered Nurse in a large California hospital for over twenty-five years. She has now taken the leap to writing full-time, but still volunteers at her local community hospital. After writing the book of her heart in 2000, she discovered the wonderful world of Mills & Boon® Medical™ Romance, where she feels the freedom to write the stories she loves. She is happily married, has two fantastic grown children, and a socially challenged rescued dog. Besides her passion for writing Medical™ Romance, she loves to travel and read. Thanks to the family dog, she takes long walks every day!

To find out more about Lynne, please visit her website: www.lynnemarshallweb.com

**Recent titles by this author:**

THE CHRISTMAS BABY BUMP
THE HEART DOCTOR AND THE BABY
THE BOSS AND NURSE ALBRIGHT
TEMPORARY DOCTOR, SURPRISE FATHER

**These books are also available in eBook format from www.millsandboon.co.uk**

## Praise for
## Lynne Marshall:

**TEMPORARY DOCTOR, SURPRISE FATHER**

'A touching, tender and engrossing Medical™ Romance,
TEMPORARY DOCTOR, SURPRISE FATHER
is a wonderful story which I devoured in a single sitting!
Don't miss this talented storyteller's enchanting tale
of second chances, devastating secrets
and the redeeming power of love!'
—*CataRomance.com*

'Lynne Marshall's excellent writing skills
lend excitement and credibility to this story…
The tension between Jan and Beck is realistic, and
keeps you reading to the very end. A very satisfactory end!'
—*The Pink Heart Society Reviews*

## DEDICATION

Heartfelt thanks to Sally, for keeping in touch and
encouraging me, and to Sheila for welcoming me back.

Also, special thanks to my daughter Emily,
for being my first reader on this book,
and for her input regarding Boston.

# CHAPTER ONE

KASEY waved toward Vincent Clark in the clinic hallway. A baby cried in the background. "Room three," she said. "Mrs. Gardner needs the second shot in her hepatitis B series."

Nine in the morning and already the small clinic's waiting room was full. A newborn needed his six-week examination; a toddler's allergies were flaring up with spring and the coming grass season; a teenage mother needed counseling on diet; a senior citizen's diabetes wasn't under control. On and on went the list, making Kasey wish she had forty-eight hours in her day.

Although today she welcomed the non-stop regimen and distractions.

"I'll get right on it," Vincent said, grabbing his laptop, flashing his killer smile.

She forced a phony grin, since smiling was the last thing she felt like doing. He deserved no less, and she didn't believe in dumping her foul mood on others. Charming, bright and sensitive, not to mention well groomed and fit, Vincent was everything Kasey looked for in a man, or used to, anyway. The catch was *she* wasn't her RN and assistant clinic administrator's type, because he was gay.

Besides, she'd given up on finding Mr. Right. Her

last big love had told her he loved her one weekend and the next said that whatever he'd said last week he didn't feel any more. What was a girl supposed to do with that? In reality, men had never stuck around for her or her mother. Since good old Arnie had broken her heart two years ago, her motto had been to keep it superficial all the way—no investment; no pain. It wasn't everything she'd hoped for in life, but it would have to do.

Vincent patted her shoulder as he passed. They adored each other in a strictly platonic way, the perfect working situation, and he was a good friend, one she could depend on. Since she'd put so much time and energy into her job over the last few years, she could count her friends on two fingers, sad but factual. As an RN, she believed in facts.

Besides, she wasn't in the market for a partner, and had given up looking, especially now, since she'd gotten the horrible news about her birth father. What would be the point of getting involved with anyone for the long haul?

She dashed to her desk to look for the notes on the toddler she'd seen last week, and found six more patient messages.

What would Vincent think if he knew her prognosis? Maybe, if things ever slowed down today, she'd tell him. No. Not here. Not quickly over a cup of coffee in the lunch room. She'd need an entire night over drinks and dinner to work up the nerve to say what frightened her more than anything on earth. But she needed to tell somebody, and soon, or she'd explode, and she needed to build her support system. She definitely needed more than two friends, especially as one lived out of state.

She let out a quiet breath and picked up a note from her receptionist and read, "*Facial laceration*", then grabbed her laptop and strode toward room one. As long as she was married to the community clinic, there'd be no chance of making new friends.

Laurette Meranvil was a name she hadn't seen before. After knocking, she opened the door and found a petite, brightly dressed woman sitting on the examination table, holding a cloth to her cheek. Kasey put her computer on the stand then reached for and shook the lady's free hand.

"I'm Kasey McGowan, the nurse practitioner. What seems to be the problem?"

"I cut my cheek on glass," the woman said with what Kasey had come to recognize as a Haitian accent.

Gingerly removing the cloth, Kasey discovered a jagged cut dangerously close to the woman's eye and extending out over her cheek. Fresh blood oozed with the release of pressure. She donned gloves and checked for obvious glass slivers in the wound but didn't find any.

"How did this happen?"

Kasey read the hesitation in the patient's eyes before the woman glanced at the floor. So often the truth went untold at the clinic. "I fell into a glass door."

Kasey ground her molars and hid her disbelief. Not that it couldn't happen, but… It was more important to treat the wound, knowing she might never get to the truth.

Though she was trained to suture, this facial laceration would leave an ugly scar if not expertly handled. Kasey knew her limitations, and the woman deserved the best treatment possible.

"Ms. Meranvil, would you be able to stay at the clinic a bit longer while I have one of the plastic surgeons from the Mass General hospital stitch your wound?" She was aware that keloids could develop at the site of the scar, and because it was on the patient's face Kasey didn't want to take any chances of disfiguring the patient even more, so she wanted to bring in an expert.

Laurette drew her eyebrows together. "I cannot pay for special treatment."

"This is the community clinic, remember? There won't be an extra charge."

After a moment's thought, Laurette gave a serious-faced nod.

"Great. We'll take you to the treatment room and get the RN to clean your wound while we wait." Kasey carefully pressed the skin flap closed and put a sterile four-by-four over it to catch the slow flow of blood then discarded her gloves and entered a quick note into the computer. "The nurse will be right with you, but in the meantime keep light pressure on it," she said, signing off and grabbing the laptop on her way out.

Once back at her desk, she found her co-worker sorting another stack of patient messages.

"Vincent, can you clean the wound in room one, give her a tetanus shot, and move her to the procedure room? I've got to make a call to see who's taking plastics call this month." As a nearby training hospital, Tufts regularly sent medical students to volunteer at the clinic, but this wound called for extra special care.

She went straight to her desk and dialed the long-memorized number of the massive teaching hospital. It supported the Everett neighborhood community clinic by supplying residents on call in various specialties as needed. After going through the usual chain of command, Kasey reached the department of surgery and was promised a second-year plastics fellowship doctor would be at the clinic within the hour. Just when she'd gotten used to last month's doctor, a bubbly young woman, May rolled around and she'd have to readjust to yet another face and name and, most importantly, personality. But that was the name of the game when operating a community clinic with a limited budget that got scrutinized with a magnifying glass each month by the trustees. She took what she was given and smiled gratefully. Fortunately, the hospital thrived on the extra experience for their interns, residents and doctor specialists in training.

After hanging up the phone and on her way to see another patient, Kasey peeked in on Laurette, noting Vincent had done a fine job of cleaning and dressing the wound. The patient rested on the gurney, staring at the ceiling, the head of the bed partially elevated.

"Can I get you some water?" Kasey asked.

The woman nodded. "Yes, thank you."

If only Kasey were a mind reader, a skill not taught in the Master's in Nursing program, maybe she could find out how the accident had really happened. Once the young woman took the water and sipped, she closed her eyes, sending the message loud and clear: I'm not talking about it. So Kasey quietly left the procedure room.

As the other examination rooms filled up, Kasey became involved with patient care, physicals and treatments, and an hour and a half later she glanced at her watch and stole a moment to get back to the nursing station.

Just about to call again, a shadow covered her desk.

She glanced up to find deep blue masculine eyes staring at her from beneath brown brows, and the hair on her neck prickled. The strikingly serious eyes studied her as if she'd come from another planet. Dark brown hair swept back from a high forehead and curled just beneath his earlobes suggesting a professional haircut hadn't found a date on his calendar in a couple of months. A day's growth of red-tinged beard covered the man's sharp jaw.

"You have a patient for me?" The quiet baritone voice sent more chills down her arms, throwing her off track and making her a little ticked off as he hadn't bothered to introduce himself yet.

Needing to look away, Kasey glanced over the man's shoulder at Vincent who, in his usual playful way, watched wide-eyed, biting his knuckle over the hunk, and she tried not to roll her eyes. Vincent was a sucker for a handsome face, and with this man Vincent's assessment was right on target. Too bad the doctor's impatient expression ruined the effect.

"Oh, um, yes, I do have a patient for you. That is if you're the resident from Plastic Surgery."

To be honest, she'd expected someone younger, more in keeping with the third—and fourth-year residents who'd normally been sent to the clinic, not a man who looked as if he'd been practicing medicine for a decade and had early signs of gray sprinkled at his temples to prove it.

He gave a slow nod, his haunting eyes as steady as a surgeon's hands, making her feel edgy. She didn't need any help with that edgy feeling today.

"I'm Jared Finch," he said.

*Snap out of it, girl.* "Hi, I'm Kasey, and over there is my co-worker, Vincent."

Vincent beamed, more gums than teeth showing. "Hi, thanks for coming."

"Just doing my job," he said, nodding hello to Vincent before turning back to Kasey. "Are you in charge?"

Unable to break away from his gaze, she fought the hitch in her breath and mentally kicked herself for falling apart. He was just a man. A doctor. She'd seen plenty of handsome men in her life, just not here in her clinic. And this man, in ten seconds flat, seemed to have absconded with her composure. She wanted to grab a rubber reflex hammer and pound some sense into her head.

"Yes. I'm the nurse practitioner and I run the clinic. Thanks so much for coming, Dr. Finch." He reached for a quick handshake, though his felt barely alive, and she shook once then let go. Even lackluster, the fraction of a moment's connection had left her off balance. *He came for the patient, give him the information.* Right. She looked through the mess on her desk, found the note, and handed it to him. Clutching the laptop that had Laurette Meranvil's information on it tightly to her chest and feeling fortified, she stood. "Let me show you the patient."

Jared followed the skittish NP down the hall toward the patient examination room. He'd been up all night, moonlighting, and the last thing he'd wanted to do was rush over to a satellite clinic for more work. Part of his commitment to the two-year plastic surgery certification program was volunteering at clinics such as this, all over town. During the month of May, as long as he wasn't doing surgery with his mentors, he'd be at the beck and call of the Everett community clinic, and would be required to put in twenty hours' service. It wasn't a "get" to, it was a "got" to, something he'd have to endure.

The nurse practitioner flipped her dark blonde hair over her shoulder and glanced at him just before opening the door. Since beginning his plastic surgery fellowship, he'd gotten into the habit of looking at women and deciding how he could improve their features. He studied the arch of her brows and the almond-shaped green eyes, the larger-than-average nose with a bump on the bridge, and her lips, small, but nicely padded. Her loose lab coat and scrub pants hid her shape, but he guessed she was at least five feet six.

"Let me show you what we've got," she said, with a polite office smile. It was nice to see she hadn't used Botox, as he preferred expressive eyes.

The corner of his mouth twitched as he followed her inside, and that would have to suffice for a friendly smile these days.

"The patient says she fell against a glass door."

He lifted one brow and shared a knowing look with the nurse practitioner as she opened the computer and brought up the patient's chart. He quickly read over her shoulder, just enough to fill him in.

"Mrs. Meranvil, I'm Dr. Finch. Let's have a look at that cut." After he'd washed his hands and donned gloves, he removed the gauze and examined the depth of the wound and potential tissue damage. "Set up a sterile field," he said to the NP, "and I'll inject some anesthetic. Do you have a tendency to develop keloids?"

The quiet woman's pinched forehead clued him to rephrase his question. "Do you get bumpy scars?"

She shook her head, and he wondered if she'd completely understood him. He glanced over her skin for any evidence of old scars to compare, but her long-sleeved, frayed-at-the-cuffs blouse didn't reveal anything.

The nurse practitioner hustled to set up the pre-sterilized pack, and he switched to sterile gloves from the basic tray then gestured to her. "I'll need five-zero polypropylene sutures."

She rustled through the cupboard until she found exactly what he wanted, opened the sterile pack and dropped it onto the sterile field. He nodded his thanks.

"Let's get started," he said, nodding toward the anesthetic. Using sterile technique, she handed him antiseptic cleanser and the tiny-gauge needle and syringe. He swiped the rubber stopper as she held the bottle upside down, and he withdrew a couple of ccs, then discarded the first needle and switched to the next, which the nurse extended to him from within its sterile wrapper.

"You'll feel a little pinch." He injected into the subcutaneous fat around the laceration as gingerly as possible. Once the effect set in, he'd look more closely for glass slivers or debris in the wound, though the nurse had cleaned it well.

Since he was up close, he gave a tight-lipped, woefully out-of-practice smile. The patient barely responded.

"Are you okay?" the nurse named Kasey asked. The patient nodded.

Right, he should employ some light banter. He cleared his throat. "Need anything?" It came out sterner than he'd meant. The patient shook her head as if afraid to talk to him.

That was the limit of his bedside manner these days, a fact he was gravely aware of and which, considering the field he was going into, needed to change. In his own good time. He took the delicate-toothed forceps and a small curved needle holder and began his meticulous suturing.

Suturing was nothing new to him—he'd been a practicing general surgeon for eight years before making the decision to go into plastic surgery. He almost gave a rueful laugh out loud over that thought as he sank another stitch and tied it off. He'd been forced to go into the big money specialty field after his wife had financially cleaned him out in the divorce two years ago. After all, a doctor of his skill and experience should be able to support his children and ex-wife without going broke.

He needed to think a hell of a lot more pleasant thoughts while treating this patient. She deserved his undivided attention and surgical expertise. The one thing he *was* sure of these days was his ability as a surgeon. Make that plastic surgeon.

Kasey was impressed with Dr. Finch's technique if not his bedside manner, and how he took great care with each stitch. If all went well with the healing process, Laurette would wind up with only a fine pale scar beneath her dark chocolate eye.

After the procedure was finished, she helped Laurette sit up. Vowing never to clean houses like her mother, she'd been a nurse since she was twenty-two, and four years later, when she'd become a nurse practitioner, she'd been initiated by fire when this clinic had opened. Nothing fazed her now. She'd worked with plenty of fussy doctors. Dr. Finch wasn't fussy, just particular about how he wanted things done. Showing a serious lack of bedside manner, he obviously had no intention of sticking around to reassure the patient. Task done, he'd already shoved the surgical tray aside, ripped off his gloves and was halfway to the door without a single word. At least he'd disposed of the trash and the used needles into the sharps container on his way, she'd give him that.

"Thanks, Doc," she said, tongue in cheek.

"Not a problem," he said in a gruff tone. Just before closing the door, he turned toward the patient. "Ms.

Meranvil, we'll need to see you back in four to five days to take out those sutures."

"Yes, Doctor," she whispered. "Thank you."

Slam, bam, thank you, ma'am?

"One more thing…" He popped his head back inside the exam room. "Has she had a tetanus booster?"

"Already taken care of," Kasey said, organizing the dressing. Sheesh, you'd think he could at least try to fake some patient concern! "Ms. Meranvil, I think you'll be pretty as ever after these stitches come out," she said as she lightly bandaged the wound.

After giving an encouraging smile to her patient, Kasey glanced over her shoulder. Jared had paused at the door.

"Agreed," he'd said.

Those unreadable steel-blue eyes almost responded to his flat, partial smile. Or maybe it was just a nod with a grimace? Talk about not putting your heart into it. At least he was a top-notch technician.

Yet those eyes…

Feeling pulled into his stare, she forced herself to look away, back to her task at hand, just as the door closed. "There. I think you're good to go." She patted Laurette on the arm, already planning her revenge on Dr. Finch.

Despite his lack of charm, Jared Finch's haunting eyes reappeared in her mind. There were far too many patients to tend to, so why get swept up in a remote and mysterious doctor's gaze?

There was just no point.

Jared sat at the corner desk in the clinic office, typing his electronic chart entry, when Kasey reappeared. Fortunately, she left him alone to go about his business while she shuffled reports and folders at the adjacent desk. There was nothing worse than being interrupted by a chatty person while trying to concentrate. He cast a furtive glance at her from across the room. Dressed in scrubs and a lab coat, there was no telling what kind of shape she had.

"Since you need to see this patient again next week," she said, ruining his hopes of blessed silence, "why don't we send out a flyer to the neighborhood?"

He stopped typing in mid-word. "A what?"

"A flyer. We can do a one-day surgical clinic."

He leveled her a look similar to that he gave his his son when he got out of line. Apparently it didn't register.

"You know, since you have to come back to follow up with Laurette's stitches?"

His dead stare stopped her for a moment. Ah, peace. He went back to the second half of that word in the report.

She cleared her throat. He tried to ignore it.

"You said yourself she has to come back in four to five days to have the stitches removed. What if there's a problem? Do you want to leave that woman scarred?" He hadn't sustained a dead stare this long since the last time his kids had ganged up on him about flying to a theme park in Florida. "Why not set up an open clinic for the local residents on Tuesday as you'll have to be here anyway?"

He slowly lifted his eyes, sending her another warning glance.

"Did you know there's a huge need for the underserved and minimally insured population in this area?" she said, undeterred. "And also, on the brighter side, you could chip away at some of the required hours for your month-long clinic rotation."

He didn't give a damn how good a saleswoman she

was, he just wanted her to shut up so he could finish his report and get back to the hospital. "Tell you what," he said. "I'll give you one whole day to see your clinic walk-in patients. There. You happy now?" May as well take up her suggestion and get this volunteer time out of the way as quickly as possible. Now maybe she'd be quiet.

She tossed him a don't-do-us-any-favors look before she commenced rushed clicking and clacking on the keyboard.

Yeah, he'd said the words, and they had seriously lacked enthusiasm, but he'd already gathered she was a smart cookie and wasn't about to let an opportunity like this slip by. Now maybe he could finish this consult and head out.

"I'll print up a flyer and hire some of the local boys to distribute them to the houses and on cars in the area."

"Great. Whatever. Now, could you let me finish my report?" That got a rise in her brows, and more speedy typing, as he'd hopelessly lost his train of thought about the wording in the report.

His concentration thrown out of the window, he recalled on his drive through the neighborhood that the boulevard was lined with red-brick and mortar storefronts, and had an eclectic assortment of businesses. Many looked rundown. The place probably could use a day-long walk-in surgery clinic, and the sooner he got his volunteer hours done the sooner he could get back to focusing fully on plastic surgery.

"Maybe you should post flyers in the local business windows, too," he said. "Though you may want to skip all the mortuaries—don't want to send the wrong message."

Quick to forgive, she laughed, and it sounded nice, low and husky. Almost made him smile.

"What's up with that anyway?"

"The overabundance of mortuaries?" she said. "I think it must have something to do with having a hospital in the area since the late eighteen hundreds and the odds of folks making it out alive." Unlike him, she could multitask, and never missed a beat typing and staring at the computer screen. "I guess the morticians went where they were guaranteed business. Though it does seem like overkill these days, pardon the pun."

He nodded, stretching his lips into a straight line rather than a smile, and grudgingly admitted he liked her dry wit and Boston accent. *Pah-din*. "Yeah, so I figure if I'm volunteering time for the month, like you said, I may as well make it worth everyone's while." Code for get it over with ASAP. That's what he was all about these days—meet his obligations as quickly as possible and move on. In another year he'd get his life back and begin his own private practice back home in California. Besides, he hated it when he ran out of things to do, preferring to work until he could pass out and sleep. Then work more. Anything to keep his mind occupied.

He scratched his jaw. "So I'll come at nine and work until seven—that way folks can stop by after they get off work," he said.

"Then why not make it eight p.m.? Would that work? With long commutes, some people don't get home from work until after seven."

Sure, squeeze an extra hour out of me, lady. "Fine," he said, staring at the last dangling sentence in his report.

Truth was, unless he moonlighted, he had nothing better to do with his time most nights. He sublet a basement bachelor apartment near Beacon Hill, with rented furniture and noisy pipes, paid through his nose for the privilege to live there, and after a year had yet to meet a single neighbor.

"That way you'd get half of your required volunteer hours out of the way in one day," she said.

He wanted to protest, say that wasn't the reason he'd agreed to do the all-day clinic, but she'd seen right through his tidy little plan. He cleared his throat. "Good point."

Her fingers clacked over the keyboard again. His concentration shot, he stood, crossed the room and looked over her shoulder at the screen. Within a couple of minutes she'd produced a first-rate flyer, complete with clip art of a stethoscope and all the pertinent information, clear and concise.

"What do you think?" She glanced up, their gazes connected. Up close he was struck by how green her eyes were, and that she was a natural blonde, and he wondered why it registered.

"Looks great," he said, leaning away while she pressed "Print" and stood.

She walked across the small and cluttered office to the antiquated printer to snag the first flyer. Holding the goldenrod paper like a picture for him to see, she smiled. "Not bad."

He looked her up and down before looking at the flyer. Yeah, not bad. "Guess I can't weasel out of it now."

She rewarded his honesty with a smile, a very nice smile. "Nope. I'm going to hold you to your word. We'll put one of these by the receptionist's window right now and start handing them out after lunch."

As she breezed across the room toward the connect-

ing front office in her oversized lab coat and scrubs, he
caught a scent of no frills soap and enjoyed the clean
smell, then discovered there was something else he fa-
vored about her. Unlike so many of his patients—size
four with forty-inch chests—she wasn't skinny trim.
She was sturdy and healthy looking, not like the let-
tuce-and-cilantro-eating women he saw in the plastic
surgery clinics.

"Look," he said, needing to get away before he discovered anything else he liked about her, or before she
bamboozled him into working there the entire month.
"I've got to run back to the hospital. I'll see you next
Tuesday."

Kasey hopped off the bus on her street, the rich smell
of fresh pizza from the corner ma and pa shop making her instantly hungry. She strode briskly against the
chill and drizzle toward her house, eager to take off her
shoes and relax. In a neighborhood lined with hundred-
year-old two-story houses, most divided into two units,
she lived amongst an interesting mix of people: the
working class; families and seniors; immigrants; and
Bostonians who could trace their American heritage
back for centuries. She loved her converted first-floor
apartment with hardwood floors and mustard-colored
walls, and appreciated her quiet neighbors, except for
that constantly squawking cockatiel next door. Skipping
up her front steps to get out of the drizzle, which had
now progressed to rain, she wondered if spring would
ever break through the dreary weather.

After grabbing the mail from the box on the porch,
she used her key to open the front door, immediately
disabling the alarm system. Sadly, living alone in the

city, it was a necessary expense, and one that gave her peace of mind. Well worth the cost.

She tossed her mail on the dining table on her way to the kitchen, and the corner of another letter left opened from yesterday caught her eye and brought back a wave of dread. Try as she may to put it out of her head all day, she'd failed. She needed a cool glass of water before she dared read it again. Maybe the words had changed. Maybe she'd misunderstood.

A quiet mew and furry brush against her ankle made her smile. She bent to pick up Daisy, her calico cat, who'd come out of hiding to greet her.

"What's up, Miss Daisy? Did you watch the birds today?" She thought how her cat sat perched on the back bedroom window-sill, twitching her tail for hours on end, most likely imagining leaping into the air to catch a chickadee busy with nest-building. "You want your dinner?"

After she'd fed the cat and drunk a whole glass of water, she went back to the table and picked up the letter from the Department of Health and Welfare.

*"It is with great sadness we inform you that your birth father, Jeffrey Morgan McAfee, has passed away from Huntington's disease..."*

She tossed the letter on the table, closing her eyes and taking a seat. She hadn't misread it. With elbows planted firmly on the worn walnut surface, she dropped her head into her hands and did something she rarely allowed: she felt sorry for herself.

*"We recommend you meet with a genetic counselor and set up a blood test..."*

She'd never known her father, her mother had never spoken of him, and this had been one hell of an introduction. She'd called her mother to verify her father's name last night, but had only got her message machine. Then later, Mom had called back to break the bad news. He was, in fact, her father. That's all she'd said, but Kasey intended to get the whole story one day soon.

*"Did he leave you anything in his will?"* So like Mom. Always looking for a free ride and never coming close to finding one.

*"Yeah, Mom, one doozy of an inheritance…"*

Kasey wouldn't wish the progressive, degenerative disease on anyone, yet with her birth father having and dying from it, she had a fifty percent chance of developing Huntington's. And once the symptoms began, *if* they began, which was a mind-wrenching thought in itself, there would be a tortured journey of wasting nerve cells, decreased cognition, Parkinson's-type rigidity and myriad other health issues until it took her life.

At least Mom had apologized, but how could a person make up for sleeping with the wrong guy, getting pregnant, and never seeing him again? Actions and consequences had never really figured into her mother's style of living.

She couldn't dwell on the disease. There was no point. While removing her head from her hands, her stomach protested, reminding her it had been hours since she'd eaten. She either carried the marker or she didn't, the ticking clock had already been set or it hadn't. Thinking how her ignorance had been bliss all these years, she had no control over anything, and now her life must go on just as it had before the letter had arrived.

She stood, losing her footing and having to grab the table for balance. Could it be an early symptom? Her throat went dry. Hadn't she been bumping into things more recently? She shook her head, scolding herself.

She'd always been clumsy, especially when she rushed, and she rushed all the time at work. There was no need to second-guess every misstep. She needed to eat, that was all.

And if she wanted peace of mind, all she needed to do was make an appointment and have a blood test and find out, once and for all, if she carried the defective gene. Be done with it or face it head on.

She'd been drawing blood from patients for years, never thought twice about having her own lab work done. Not since a kid had the thought of a laboratory test sent an icy chill of fear down her spine. Until today. What would she do if she had Huntington's? She tightened her jaw and stood straighter. If she had the disease, she'd just have to make the most of each day...until the symptoms began, and even then, she promised to live life to the fullest for as long as she was physically able.

Though her stomach growled a second time, she'd just lost her appetite.

# CHAPTER TWO

FRIDAY night, hidden in a booth and lost in the noise of the local Pub, Kasey took another sip of her beer. She'd asked Vincent to join her for dinner, her treat, hoping to work up the nerve to tell him her troubles. So far they'd each had a deli sandwich, hers the chicken breast, his the beef dip, and they'd shared a Caesar salad. Vincent had just ordered a second round of beer, yet she still hadn't broached the subject etched in her genes and squeezing her heart.

"O. M. G., look!" Vincent pointed to the bar with the neck of his low-calorie beer bottle. "It's him, Dr. Tall, Dark, and Gorgeous."

Kasey almost choked on her drink when her eyes focused on the broad shoulders covered in a well-cut jacket, and the trim hips and jeans-clad legs. Though from Vincent's perspective Dr. Finch might be, she wouldn't go so far as to call him tall, but somewhere more in the vicinity of five eleven or so. Why split hairs, when the conclusion was the same? The man was a hunk.

Speaking of hair, and since she was now officially living her life for the moment, waves like those gave her the urge to run her fingers through them, just to see how they felt. She glanced at Vincent and realized he was probably thinking the same thing, and it made her blurt out a laugh. They shared the same taste in men. Where Jared Finch might possess superb physical traits, he sorely lacked both personality and charm, going from the short encounter she'd had with him. Looks could only take a man so far in her opinion. Maybe she wasn't the only person in the world with problems? Kasey continued to glance toward the bar, intrigued.

"I wonder what he's doing here," she said.

"Well, duh, drinking!" Vincent reached across the booth table and patted her hands. "He must be human, just like us. Isn't that sweet?"

Vincent had been teased mercilessly all his life about his carrot-top hair, which he now kept meticulously combed and perfectly spiked, resembling a torch on top. If the red hair didn't set him apart, his alabaster-white skin dotted with free-flowing freckles sealed the deal when combined with his fastidious style of dress and precise mannerisms. He'd survived a tough childhood and now lived life exactly as he pleased. As a result he owned the sweetest content smile on the planet. Right now he shared that smile with Kasey. Sparkles beamed from his eyes—even in the darkened pub Kasey could see them—as he watched Jared standing at the bar, hoisting a mug, taking a swig and watching the Red Sox on the big screen.

"I don't think he's with anyone," Vincent said. "I'm going to invite him over." He shot out of the booth and zigzagged through the crowd before Kasey had a chance to stop him.

"Don't do that!" she said, her voice overpowered by piped-in Irish rock music as he was halfway across the bar. *"I need to talk to you...tell you my horrible news. And that guy's a real pill."*

Biting her lips, she refused to watch Vincent. Instead, she cringed, took another drink of her beer and hoped Dr. Finch had a short memory. Or that he thought Vincent was too forward and invading his privacy and refused to associate with subordinates. That would suit his attitude.

Unable to stand the suspense, she glanced from the corner of her eye toward the bar. Damn, the men were both headed for the booth. She sat straighter and fussed with her bangs, then wished she hadn't left her hair in the French braid tucked under at her nape. They'd come here straight from work, and a whole lot of hair had escaped since that morning, judging by the tendrils tickling her neck. She must look a mess, and what had been completely acceptable for spending time with Vincent would now fail miserably for making an impression on Vincent's Dr. Tall, Dark, and Gorgeous. Why should she care?

Catching an errant strand of hair and tucking it behind her ear, another pang of anxiety got her attention. What the heck was she supposed to talk about? The plan had been to wine and dine Vincent, then tell him her woes, not have a social encounter with an aloof plastic surgeon. She hated it when her plans didn't work out.

When Jared arrived at the booth, his tentative smile made her suspicious he'd had a drink or two already, since friendliness hadn't been his strong suit at the clinic. "Hi," he said. "I was just on my way out when Vinnie caught me."

Vincent preened in the background over his job well done.

"Hi, Dr. Finch, what are you doing here?" she said, ignoring her gloating friend and cringing over the lame question.

"Having a drink—what else?" He pinched his brows together and glanced around the pub just as a group of three waiters broke into song at the booth next to theirs. They sang "Happy birthday" to a young woman who didn't look a day over sixteen, though they served her a fancy umbrella drink with a flaming candle in it, so she had to be at least twenty-one. Yep, by the end of the song they'd sung, "Happy twenty-first birthday to Shauna".

"I feel so old," Jared said, after watching the celebration. "Is there an upper age limit at this bar? No one over thirty allowed?"

"Oh, no. That's not what I meant when I asked what you were doing here. What I meant was I'm just surprised to see you here, that's all." This was more of a locals bar, not a place for doctors, especially future plastic surgeons.

He sat next to her, and she scooted several inches in the other direction, though there wasn't far to go, her hands clutching the glass of pale ale. "And, besides, if the age limit is thirty, I'd be too old, too."

"You're not over thirty, are you?" He sat with a hand on each knee, back to looking stiff and out of his element.

"Thirty-two last January." She didn't care if he knew her age—she wasn't looking for his approval.

"I would have pegged you around twenty-six or -seven."

Well, then. She sat a little straighter. Yes, he was being nice, she knew it, but nevertheless he'd scored a few plus points over the unintentional compliment. His attempt to be kind was a far cry from the standoffish guy she'd met the other day.

"Now I know you've had a couple of pints." She

felt the blush from his compliment as deeply as when she'd been twelve and regularly embarrassed. How silly was that?

He stopped just before he finished off his dark brew. "From these thirty-nine-year-old eyes, you look twenty-six. Trust me."

"How old do I look?" Vincent asked, looking a little desperate to get into the game.

"Vinnie, I'm thinking twenty-four."

Vincent giggled, actually giggled. "Oh, Doctor, you're so funny, I'm thirty. And could you call me Vincent, please?"

"Apologies, Vincent. Then we're all over the hill. Good. I don't relate to the younger generation, anyway. All the face piercings and tattoos, fake boobs."

Kasey took another swallow of beer to help the dry patch in her throat as she thought about the four silver hoops in various sizes in both of her ears, the silver ball in her left tragus, the small rose tattoo hidden on her right hip, and the hummingbird on her left shoulder. Her breasts were her own, though. She sat a little straighter, thinking about it. "But you're going to be a plastic surgeon, so won't you be augmenting a lot of those 'boobs'?"

"I'm depending on it. Lots of cash in breast augmentation. And lipo. Ah, and we can't forget Brazilian butt lifts. Big bucks there, too."

He seemed too caught up with the money side of the job, and it made her subtract some of those points she'd just awarded him. Her thoughts must have shown on her face.

"There's nothing wrong with helping people look the way they want," Vincent said, practically shushing her as if she'd been rude to their guest.

"Within reason." For some crazy reason—maybe the second half of the pale ale—she wasn't ready to back down. "You wouldn't give anyone cat eyes if they asked, would you? Or a doll's nose, or pull someone's face so tight they looked like they'd just hit G-force?"

Surprising her, Jared gave a good-hearted laugh—a deep, really nice-sounding laugh, which suited his urbane appearance and classy charm. "I've often wondered if some plastic surgeons forget their oaths to do no harm." He touched her forearm, sending her focus away from his mesmerizing eyes. "You'd probably think less of me if I said, 'If the price was right', so I won't answer that question."

His dodge disappointed her, and he looked less handsome for it. Then she mentally kicked herself, wondering who was shallower, him for doing what his patients asked or her for getting all caught up in a man with an intriguing face before knowing a single thing about him.

Everyone around the table stared at their drinks. The silence had gone on long enough.

"You're not from Massachusetts, are you?" she said.

He shook his head. "California."

"What brings you out this way?" Vincent asked.

"My kids." He got a distant, almost pained look in his eyes, but quickly snapped out of it. "They go to school out here." He took a long swig of his drink. "My ex-wife insisted on sending them to an exclusive boarding school back east, which meant moving across country and driving two hours in order to see them every other weekend."

"So does your ex live here too?" Vincent asked.

"Nope. Patrice is still back in California."

This earnest dad who'd do anything, including move across the country, to be near his kids, took her by surprise. If she had been keeping tally, he'd moved back up the plus column. "I've heard it's a great school." Meaning it was expensive.

"Oh, yeah, the best." He finished another long drink. "Which is the main reason I chose plastic surgery this time around." He gave an I-don't-give-a-damn-what-you-think glance, meant only for Kasey.

Yes, he came off gruff and uncaring, and maybe a little drunk to be talking about this with near strangers, but Kasey saw through the façade and did the math. He had an ex-wife who got alimony and kids in a private school. The man was upgrading his pay scale by going into plastic surgery. A perfectly respectable specialty in this day and age so she wasn't going to come down hard on him for that.

Her father had never even tried to find her. This guy had moved across the country to be near his kids.

He took a long draw on the last of his beer. Vincent waved his hand to the passing waitress and ordered another round. "You're not driving, are you, Dr. Finch?"

"Call me Jared. Actually, I'm within walking distance of here. What about you guys?"

"The T," Kasey and Vincent answered in unison, then locked pinky fingers. "Jinx, one, two, three, you owe me a beer," they also said in unison.

Jared cocked his head, glancing at Kasey and Vincent. "I keep forgetting I'm not in California any more. We can't live without our cars." Ignoring the pinky locking, he pinned Kasey with an inquisitive look. "Do you feel safe riding the T at night?"

"As a woman, I'm never completely comfortable commuting after dark, but as long as I'm home before midnight, I'm okay with it. Anyway, after the T there's a bus that takes me right to my street corner. It works out pretty well."

Jared glanced across at Vincent. "You're not seeing her home?"

"She's my best friend, but also a big girl, and I'm a big boy in the big city. Besides, I live in Jamaica Plains at the other end of the Orange line, and she lives in Everette. We're okay with that, aren't we, Kase?"

"Yeah." She nodded, just as the waitress delivered their next round of beers. "I'm fine with that. If you can't handle the transportation, get out of the city, I always say."

From across the booth Vincent reached for a high five and she joined him, grateful she wasn't drinking on an empty stomach and wondering what the heck Dr. TD&G thought about their childish antics. Ah, what did she care? After next Tuesday he'd only have another eight to ten hours left to volunteer at the clinic and then she'd never see him again anyway.

By the end of the next beer even Jared had loosened up and the conversation had run the gamut from surviving while going to school to favorite pubs in the area to bad break-ups. And Kasey's head had started to spin with all the details.

"This certain person, who shall rename mainless," Vincent said, and giggled. "I mean shall remain nameless, took all my favorite CDs and DVDs before we broke up. Should've seen it coming, I guess."

"No, no, no." Jared said. "You have no idea what a real break-up is. California style. I've been a doctor for thirteen years and I'm living in a basement apartment with rented furniture, thanks to my ex."

"So that's why you're going into plastic surgery," Vincent said, with a poor-baby gaze in his eyes.

"Absolutely. Plus the fact I believe people should be able to look the way they want. If I can help make them happy with their appearance, I'll be glad to do it."

The man was definitely toeing the line on plastic surgery, and she was beginning to believe his sincerity.

Somewhere during the conversation Kasey had slipped into the shadows of her mind, leaving Vincent to stir up mischief and Jared willingly joining in. She'd heard the retold saga of Vincent's childhood in Kansas and what had brought him to Boston. She'd also gathered some interesting information about Jared's fifteen-year marriage to his college sweetheart, Patrice, and how over the years his ex had changed into a shopaholic, how it had ruined their marriage and caused their divorce two years ago. She also knew one-sided stories were never accurate, and wondered what the rest of that tale was. She suspected he was still hurting about the break-up of his family, and even thought about commenting on that, though didn't get that far.

With all the open conversation, Kasey hadn't managed to share a single thing about herself.

Kasey's mind slipped back to the latest news, the worst news of her life. She'd managed to distract herself the last couple of hours with the male company and pale ale, yet now it tiptoed back into her thoughts and soured her stomach.

"You're awfully quiet," Vincent prodded.

"Yeah, what about you?" Jared said. "Don't you have any dating war stories?"

She laughed and swiped at the air, her idea of feeling cavalier about life's major curve balls. "You guys don't have anything to complain about."

Vincent's cellphone rang. He checked who it was, his eyes going wide. "Speak of the devil."

Kasey faked a grin for Jared, who returned a be-
nign smile, while Vincent took the call. She tore her
bar napkin into three soggy parts while mulling over
her news. The waitress arrived, and Jared ordered for
them, though Vincent shook his head. Jared glanced at
Kasey again, one brow raised.

*Sure. What the heck. I'm living life moment to mo-
ment now, right?* She nodded, and Jared ordered for
both of them.

Vincent finished his call. "It's been great, but I've
got to go." He fished in his pocket for cash for his share
of the bar bill.

"You're leaving?" Kasey said, as in was he leaving
her there alone with Dr. Finch?

"A certain someone has come to their senses."

"Returning all the CDs and DVDs?" Jared said, surprising Kasey that he'd actually been following along.

Vincent looked startled. "Oh, good point. I'll make
sure of it." He flashed his winning smile, kissed Kasey
on the cheek, and left.

Wait! I need to talk to you!

What the heck was she supposed to do now?

Jared didn't move to the opposite side of the table,
which made a little knot form in her stomach. The waitress brought the drinks and he paid, not giving Kasey
a chance to chip in. The tummy knot got tighter. When
the server left, he raised his glass to her and took a
drink. She joined him.

This socializing business could get long and painful, trying to be polite and having absolutely nothing
to talk about. Or he'd finish his drink and get up and
leave, and could she blame him Someone had to start
a conversation, so it may as well be her.

"What are your kids' names?"

"Chloe and Patrick." His face immediately lit up. "She's ten and he's twelve. Great kids." He got out his smartphone and found their pictures. She admired the bright smiles and happy eyes. Both children had their father's eyes.

"You have kids?" he asked.

"No. I'm not married." Well, that hadn't stopped her mother.

He sat for a few moments, pondering her answer. "So tell me," he said, "what was it like, growing up in Boston?"

Yeah, they really didn't have a thing to talk about.

"Actually, I'm a south shore girl. I grew up in Kingston, which is close to Plymouth. My mom and I lived with my grandmother." She left out the part about her mom cleaning houses for the rich ladies of Duxbury, and how she could never afford to move the two of them out on their own. "I guess it's like growing up any other place."

"What does 'south shore' mean?"

"That I grew up south of Boston. Now, I guess, since I had the opportunity to open the community clinic and move to Everett, you could call me a 'north shore' girl."

He gave her a blank stare. She was failing miserably as a pub buddy.

"In my heart I'll always be a south shore girl, I guess." She wanted to squirm, his lack of interest was so noticeable. What was the first rule of socialization? People loved to talk about themselves. Ask him a question.

"What part of California are you from?"

"L.A."

"Are you the only doctor in your family?"

"Yes. Mom was a teacher and Dad ran a small business in Echo Park. My brother's a fireman."

So he hadn't come from money, like she'd assumed. See, asking questions always helped break the ice.

They chatted about his upbringing, having to yell back and forth in order to be heard over the ever-increasing Friday-night crowd at the pub as they finished their drinks.

"You feel like some coffee?" he said. "The noise is getting to me."

Surprised by his invitation, she nodded. "Sounds good." She wasn't ready to be alone with her morbid thoughts, which had subsided while engaged in small talk with Jared.

Jared watched Kasey as she exited the pub. She'd worn straight-legged jeans rolled up at the ankles, candy-apple red flats, a matching blouse with ruffles down the front, which accentuated her bust, and an oatmeal-colored extra-long sweater with the sleeves pushed up to her elbows. The street lights made all the loose hair around her head look like a halo. He liked the shape of her face, didn't even mind the batch of earrings on both ears or the Boston accent. It was cute and not whiny, like some of the women he'd heard since moving east. Maybe it had to do with the south-shore versus north-shore girl bit, but what did he know?

She was different from most women he'd been around lately, too. After giving it some thought, he decided it was because of a decided lack of pretentiousness. She seemed grounded, wanted to work with the folks who needed her the most, and she wasn't seduced by the almighty dollar like so many people in his life. Hell, like him.

Two doors down he found the local coffee bar, and held the door open for her. She seemed a little unstable on her feet—maybe he shouldn't have bought her that last beer—so he guided her by the elbow to an empty table. "What do you drink?"

She rattled off her latte order, tagging on fat-free milk. He made the order and waited for the drinks while she went to the bathroom. When they met up back at the table, he could tell she'd brushed her hair and put on more lipstick, and wondered if she'd done it for him. The thought, whether true or not, pleased him.

They shared a few sips of coffee in silence. She seemed tense, and he figured it was because she felt stuck with him. He didn't feel the same. In fact, he was glad to have someone to talk to and wished he could make her relax. Truth was, if she couldn't settle down after a couple of beers, there was no helping her.

"I got some pumpkin bread," he said. "Want to share?"

She smiled and took half. "Thanks." She was generous with her smiles, and he liked that.

"Can I get your opinion about something?" he said, just before popping a pinch of bread into his mouth.

She blew over her cup and nodded. "Sure."

"Do you think little girls should be allowed to dress like small adults?"

Obviously, this wasn't the turn she'd expected the conversation to take. She pulled in her chin and thought for a second or two. "No. As a matter of fact, I resent little kids looking better in the latest styles than I do."

"Yeah, well, I'm glad my kids' private school has a dress code, because sometimes I think Chloe's taste in clothes is far beyond her years."

"Sounds like a sore spot."

"Yeah. I don't like to argue with her about it. As long as she dresses within reason, I'm okay, but sometimes she looks like a tiny adult." He grinned. "That's when I pull out the phone and take her picture, text it to my ex and let her weigh in on the outfit. If she approves, I keep my trap shut, but sometimes, well, let's just say I miss my girl in her overalls and flowered T-shirts, you know?"

He wasn't trying to impress Kasey or anything, but he caught a look of longing in her eyes, as if she really dug guys who worried about their daughters. "It wasn't my idea," he said, noticing a touch of confusion in her expressive eyes. "The divorce."

"So you didn't divorce purely on shopaholic grounds?" Her knowing gaze told him he hadn't fooled her for a minute back at the bar.

He offered a humble smile. "Maybe the fact I was never around, always working on developing my private practice, had something to do with her turning to shopping. I guess it filled a void but, damn, practically every penny I made she spent."

"Did you guys seek counseling?"

He nodded. "Too little, too late. I wish my ex well and all, I'd just like to have more say in my kids' lives."

"You *should* have input since you're their dad."

He gave her an earnest smile before he took another drink. She seemed surprised by it, with a quick yet subtle double-take before returning his smile.

"Thanks for being honest," she said, popping another bite of pumpkin bread into her mouth. "We've all got problems. Sometimes we need to get them off our chest. Not that I'm asking you to unload all your gripes about your ex on me or anything."

He laughed. "No-o-o, I wouldn't do that. I'm sure she's got her share of gripes, too."

"Again, thanks." She took a dainty sip and he really liked watching her, making him wonder what was up with that.

"You seem pretty well set up. No husband. No kids. You get to run a busy clinic. Make a differ—" Her laser-sharp stare stopped him in mid-word. "What?"

"I just found out I have a fifty-fifty chance of developing Huntington's," she said, with a defiant, subtly quivering smile.

Why she had let her dark secret slip out to Jared, she had no clue. Maybe it was because he'd opened up about his family and his frustrations as a father. Or because he tried to make her life sound all rosy-toes. From her perspective at least his problems were fixable. Maybe it was because she needed to get the burden of truth off her chest, and Vincent wasn't around, and tonight was the night she'd planned to tell him. Whatever the reason, she'd said it, quite out of the blue, and from the sinking in her stomach, wished she could take it back, or at least stop her eyes from welling up. Darn it. The last thing she wanted to do was go all emotional on him. Not here. Not in public.

His gaze went stone cold, his body rigid. Dead silence ensued. Kasey could have sworn the coffee-bar music, which was quiet compared to the bar, got turned down ten more notches.

She knew the second the words had slipped out of her mouth she'd made a huge mistake. This wasn't how she'd planned to tell someone. She'd wanted to tell Vincent, cry on his shoulder, let him soothe her, not tell a man she'd only just met. She'd never had any intention of telling Dr. Finch!

It was too late to take back the words and, oh, God, the look on his face, his startled gaze, was more than she could bear. She didn't want his sympathy. The truth of the matter was she'd needed to tell someone before she exploded and now that she'd said it she couldn't take it back.

Jared leaned in and looked at her with sad and serious eyes. "Wouldn't you have already known if one of your parents had the disease?"

"Just got word my father died from it. I never knew him. Listen, I didn't mean to say that. I certainly didn't mean to hijack the conversation, but…"

Jared clamped his hand on her forearm. "This is tough news. You should've told me to shut the hell up with all my trivial griping. Have you taken the blood test yet?"

She shook her head.

"You need to have that test. You'll go crazy with worry until you know for sure."

"Tell me about it," she said. "I found out three days ago, and I can barely function."

"I'm surprised you've lasted this long! Listen, we've got a great genetic research department, I'll arrange for you to have the test ASAP."

"I can get it done…"

"Let me help you," Jared said. "Now is no time to flaunt your big-girl panties. I get it that you're an independent, big-city woman raised by a single parent, and you can handle everything by yourself, but just this once why not let someone else help you out?"

Was that what he'd taken away from their conversation tonight? That she was hard-headed and fiercely independent? Right now she felt anything but. Or maybe he saw her as impossibly stubborn. Either way, she was shutting him out with her response.

Hadn't she recently given herself a lecture about needing more than two friends? The man had just offered to help her out. She should take it and be grateful.

"Okay." She glanced at Jared and forced a smile. "Thanks. Let me know when to have the blood drawn and where to go."

"I'll get right on it first thing Monday." He removed his hand from her arm and she immediately missed the warmth. He withdrew his cellphone and entered a note. "Maybe Vincent can go with you for moral support."

She nodded her thanks. "That's a thought." She really didn't want to go through this alone, and having Vincent's support would mean the world to her, that was when she finally had a chance to tell him. Who would have thought she'd first blurt out her news to a near stranger?

"Oh, and another thing," Jared said, putting his phone away.

She looked into his steady, concerned gaze.

"You're not riding the T home by yourself tonight. I'm coming with you."

After a brisk walk a couple of blocks to the station, they entered to the T. She didn't even have to open her wallet to use her magnetic card to open the gate. Being from California, the whole public transportation thing still amused Jared. Seeing him fiddle in his pockets, searching for his Charlie card, she handed him her wallet.

"Here, you can use mine. I've got a bundle on it."

"Thanks." He took it and placed it over the card reader, waiting for the blip and the gate to pop open. Once inside, they rushed towards the red line, heading for Ashmont. She knew what she was doing, had probably ridden this line a thousand times. He followed along, making mental notes to do the reverse when it was time to go home.

She strode along, looking the picture of health and confidence, yet she'd been delivered a blow that would have brought most people to their knees. Huntington's. Man, oh, man.

Granted there was a fifty percent chance she wouldn't have the marker and develop the symptoms, and he hoped that would be the case, but it was still a raw deal. She seemed in her prime and deserved all that life could give her. It simply wasn't fair.

She glanced back as if to make sure he was keeping up, and her soft smile and friendly eyes tugged at his heart. She'd gone from mere business associate to a woman who needed protecting in one evening, and though it was the last thing he wanted to get involved in—he had enough going on already—he felt compelled to be there for her.

Crazy. Absolutely crazy. He hardly knew her. It wasn't his style. He had enough people depending on him already. Surely she had other friends and family around. At least there was Vincent. Yeah, Vincent would be there for her.

She'd never known her father, and didn't seem to be close to her mother. At least that was what he'd gathered from their conversation tonight. She needed a friend, that's all. Was that so much to ask? Yes, as a matter of fact, it was. Relationships of any kind were definitely out for him at this stage as he was still smarting from the divorce. He glanced at her again and felt a firm yank on his heart. Aw, hell, maybe he should make the effort to be a friend before he forgot how it felt. Could he even do "friend" any more?

Did he really want to be a friend? Being a friend meant having a friend. So far, other than medical professionals, he didn't have a single friend in Boston, and it had suited him just fine. Except for when he wanted to go to a Sox game and didn't have anyone to go with, or when he didn't feel like eating alone. Again.

Train fumes invaded his nostrils, a street musician played classical guitar in the corner. A thick crowd of people pushed toward the automatic doors on the train as they opened. He strode in front of her and helped her on board, guiding her at the small of her back. He thought he saw a flicker of surprise in her glance as she boarded. Her eyes were soft and green, and, as hard as he tried not to, he liked them.

Once the doors closed, and they'd both grabbed a pole to hang onto, she looked at him. "What a coincidence, seeing you at the pub tonight."

Should he tell her he couldn't stand the thought of going home to his empty apartment to eat alone on a Friday night? "I heard they had great pastrami sandwiches and I wanted to watch the Sox game because they played the Los Angeles Angels."

She nodded. Maybe she believed him, maybe not. "I love their deli food, too. Do you go there often?"

"Once in a while." Hey, she'd been brutally honest with him, the least he could do was be honest back. With a look of chagrin, he started. "Truth is I hit that pub every other Friday night, same routine. Pastrami. Beer. Ball game. The other weekends I have visitation rights with my kids. Then I head out to the school and stay overnight at a motel so I'll be there bright and early to take my kids for breakfast on Saturday morning."

She looked at him more closely now, as if grateful he'd told the truth. "Very interesting. And to think I thought doctors all hung out in fancy restaurants, having doctorly conversations on Friday nights."

She'd forced a smile out of him, and he shook his head at the upside-down logic. Under the dreary circumstances, *he* should be the one trying to make *her* smile.

At the first stop, a large group of people got off, and they had the option to sit, but Kasey stayed standing so Jared did too.

"Does your mom still live in Boston?" he asked.

"No. She lives in Nevada. Works in one of the casinos." She scratched her nose. "Since my nana died, I don't have any relatives nearby."

No support system whatsoever. That had to hurt.

"But I've got Vincent. He's my best buddy these days."

Vincent was her closest friend, and Jared was glad for that. "That's it?"

"My other best friend, Cherie, moved to New York, so we don't get to hang out as much as we used to."

Something about the matter-of-fact way she'd admitted to being almost completely on her own pulled at him. Made him want to do right by her, which proved he'd had one beer too many, and that was that.

Downtown they got off and headed for the orange line toward Oak Grove. He made another mental note for the trip back home.

Whether she knew it or not, she needed looking after, and against his far better judgment, judgment that would normally have him running in the opposite direction, he saw a person who deserved to have a friend during this tough time. So he made a snap decision to sign on for the job. It wasn't like he had to be her best friend or anything, just keep an eye out for her, make sure she got to the lab and followed up after the results. Hell, the last thing he could handle in his life right now was a new friend with a debilitating disease. Truth was he'd be useless as a friend. He needed to put all his energy into being a good dad. There just wasn't enough left over for anything else.

Aw, what the hell.

Once Kasey and Jared exited the T they were lucky enough to find Kasey's bus waiting out front and hopped right on. She'd grown noticeably quiet, and hoped he didn't interpret it as not wanting him around. She'd been touched by his offer to see her home. Within ten minutes they were at her corner stop and jumped off.

"This is my street. I live five houses down on the right. Mission accomplished." She stepped back and slipped off the curb.

He grabbed her elbow to balance her.

"You don't want me to walk you home?" he said as they crossed the street.

"Thanks. I'm good. Really."

She felt completely out of his league, and it was partially because of his aristocratic air, as if coming from California and riding the T was a big adventure for a guy like him, rubbing elbows with the folks and all. But he'd told her his mother was a teacher and his father a small businessman. Hardly aristocracy. Must be the overly confident surgeon part of his personality coming across.

She'd spilled her guts about the Huntington's so he probably felt obligated to look after her. Well, she didn't need his pity. Not now. Not ever.

He pocketed his hands, waiting.

Maybe she'd been too abrupt, but what was the point?
He insisted on following her home, and she was grateful for that, but she didn't need him walking her right
to the door.

He couldn't possibly have something like seduction
in mind could he? Would he be so crass to take advantage of a woman who'd just admitted she might have
Huntington's? Unfortunately, she'd dated a guy or two
like that in her life.

She glanced at him, passively waiting for her directions. No. That wasn't it.

They'd reached the other side of the street and Kasey
had a decision to make. Let the man walk her to her
house and then what? Scurry to pick up the breakfast
dishes or discarded clothing from the living room? Feel
like she had to offer him something, and not sure she
had a single soda in the fridge? Had she left her bra on
the sofa?

Or she could stay with him here until the next bus
back to the T arrived. Wouldn't that be the practical
thing to do?

"Wow, that pizza smells great," he said, leaning back
and noticing the Mama's pizza parlor neon sign. "I'd
weigh three hundred pounds if I lived this close."

"The novelty wears off as the scale goes up, believe
me."

He half smiled, genuine and warm, and it halted
her breathing for an instant. Maybe she had pegged
him all wrong.

"Doesn't seem to have done any damage to you—
you look fine just the way you are."

Ah, a smooth talker. Maybe he did have seduction
plans.

Did a girl with a crooked nose, an ordinary face, and

ample hips really look fine just the way she was to a future plastic surgeon? If her ex, the guy who'd broken her heart into pieces, hadn't been able to accept her the way she was, a man like Jared would probably never waste a minute on someone like her. Didn't he fix people like her? Maybe he did feel sorry for her. Well, no way would she tolerate someone feeling sorry for her, even if he did look sexy as hell standing under that neon sign. Sexy *and* kissable.

What in the world was she thinking, and why did he cause her to have these thoughts?

Oh, hell, this was too confusing, and the last thing she needed was to be confused tonight.

She noticed the bus lights coming down the street with great relief. "There's the bus back to the T station. You'd better hop on because they come a lot less frequently this time of night."

"I'd rather make sure you made it *all the way* home," he said, grabbing her arm and squeezing, making her wonder what his version of "all the way home" meant. Did he think she was an easy hit, that he'd be doing her a favor to seduce her in her time of need?

Though fundamentally wrong, she also saw the upside of grabbing life by the horns and riding it for all it was worth, especially now, with her future at stake. But not tonight. Not with Jared. Neither of them had any business getting involved with each other.

"Really. I'm fine." She pointed down the street. "Count down five houses and see that big bronze star on the top floor? That's me. I live downstairs. Got a guard cat waiting and everything. Go," she said as the bus pulled up with a screeching of brakes. "You've done your gentlemanly duty for the night."

He didn't immediately let go of her arm, and gazed

into her eyes so deeply she felt her toes twitch. "I'm calling the lab first thing Monday morning about that blood test. I'll be in touch as soon as I have a date for you."

"Thanks. I really appreciate it." She did, too.

"Which means you'll need to give me your phone number and address."

She rattled off her numbers as he entered it into his phone. "Got it."

He nodded, smiling and watching her, and there was nothing else he could say. Not now. Not until the test was done and the results were in.

The bus door opened.

"I'll see you Tuesday at the clinic," he said, getting on the bus.

She didn't have a chance to respond, but stood and watched as the bus pulled off. Waving briefly, she turned and headed home, seriously hoping he wouldn't forget about making the appointment for the blood tests. After all, she hardly knew the man, so why should he care?

She kept a brisk pace in the cool night, avoiding an overturned trash can and a car in a driveway blocking the sidewalk.

Of all the crazy times to meet a man who intrigued her, a man who turned her on with his dark hair and crystal-blue stare. A man who seemed a little interested in her, too. She shook her head, not believing that part of the equation. At least from the way he'd sat close to her in the bar when there had clearly been room to stretch out, and on the T, how he'd guided her by lightly touching the small of her back when they'd got on and off. Did he have a clue how heady that gesture was?

This was all too confusing. She needed to get a grip, think things through. Jared had changed from an aloof surgeon into a halfway nice guy tonight, but she didn't do halfway nice guys any more. That's how she'd gotten her heart ripped out of her chest the last time. She'd believed her halfway nice guy when he'd told her he loved her. The problem was, Mr. Halfway-Nice hadn't convinced himself about love. If love meant sticking around, being there through the rough patches, he'd failed miserably. Why would Jared Finch be any different?

She shook her head, remembering her plan B. Superficial. Keep all future male-female relationships superficial. But that had been before she'd found out about her father and Huntington's. Should she think about any relationships at all until she knew her results?

Jared's handsome face popped into her thoughts again. He was a man who seemed like he could use some unattached companionship just as much as she could. Too bad she wasn't in the mood for an affair.

# CHAPTER THREE

TUESDAY morning, Kasey arrived at the free clinic a half-hour early to find a line of people halfway down the block waiting out front.

"Good morning, everyone," she called out. "Please be patient today." She hoped everyone at the end of the line heard her. "We'll work as quickly as we can." She let herself in the door, locking it behind her. The clinic wasn't due to open until nine a.m.

She went to her desk, booted up the computer and went about her morning chores. Dr. Finch hadn't called on Monday as he'd said he would. So much for getting swept up in his promises and dreamy looks. She should have known better since men had a long record of letting her down, beginning with her absent father, her mother's long list of deadbeat boyfriends, and ending with her own string of sour relationships.

With the special clinic today, she'd be too busy to do research on labs that would be able to do special genetic studies, but she promised herself she'd tackle it first thing tomorrow.

What if Dr. Finch didn't show up today? It hadn't exactly been his idea, but he'd agreed. Her stomach tightened at the thought of having to explain to all of the patients their clinic would have to be cancelled because the future plastic surgeon hadn't kept his promise.

She snapped her fingers. If he did show up, they'd be short a computer unless he brought his laptop. Why hadn't she remembered to tell him that? Was it too late to call him? A sudden blast of nerves had her flitting all over the nurses' station, searching for his phone number, not even sure she had it.

Vincent arrived through the back door in powder-blue scrubs, his lab jacket over his arm and hair sculpted in several directions. "Wow, we'll be here until tomorrow, seeing all of those patients."

"I know," she said, distracted with checking supplies. "Good thing we set up all the rooms last night. Is Angie here yet?" Angie, the ready-to-retire receptionist and medical assistant, was notorious for being late to work.

"She was parking when I got here." Vincent headed straight for the coffee pot, found a filter and held up the can of coffee, shaking it to emphasize it was almost empty as the back door opened. "Do we have a grocery list going? We need coffee and powdered creamer."

"What we need," she said, "is that doctor to show up."

"Got it, and present," said a familiar masculine voice.

Kasey glanced up to find Jared standing with a take-out tray of steaming coffees in one hand and a brown bag in the other. A mini-cringe made her cheeks warm. He wore a tan suede jacket over a button-down pin-striped yellow shirt, pressed denim jeans and brown loafers. *Who pressed their jeans*? He hadn't forgotten to bring his laptop either, as a stylish computer case hung from his shoulder.

"Oh, hi," she said, glancing at his face then her desk,

feeling embarrassed. Even from this distance, his freakishly blue eyes did things to her she wasn't prepared for.

"You're a god," Vincent said, rushing to his aid. "Good morning, and I'll take these, thank you very much."

"Don't thank me, thank Angie."

Vincent grabbed the coffees and passed them out to Kasey and Angie, who'd entered behind Jared. "Thank you, Ms. Angie, and here's one for you." He handed Jared his coffee. "And one for me."

"Yes, thank you, Angie," Kasey said, wondering what had prevented Jared from getting back to her yesterday about the lab appointment.

He handed the brown bag back to Angie.

She held it up. "These bagels were fresh from the oven when I picked them up at the bakery forty minutes ago," Angie said.

"From that line I saw circling around the block, we're going to need carbs and lots of them, so thanks," Jared said, being the first to be offered a bagel.

"How sweet," Vincent said, finding a blueberry bagel and taking a huge bite.

When the cream cheese made an appearance, Kasey sauntered over, though not wanting to get too close to Jared, leery that his sexual gravity might snag her like a magnet. She took a sesame bagel, smearing it with strawberry flavored soft cheese, then savored the fresh-bread smell as she gobbled it down. A simple pleasure on what promised to be a hellishly busy day. From the corner of her eye she noticed Jared watching her as she licked away the cream cheese at the corner of her mouth.

For distraction, Kasey ticked off a list of items for Angie to stock in the patient rooms then sipped her hot, rich coffee. She'd keep today's visit from Dr. Finch strictly business, which it was. Though it had been her idea to run this clinic, he'd be expected to take charge of the lion's share of the patients. At least he'd showed up, that was a start. If all went well, after today she wouldn't have to see him again for the rest of the month.

Grabbing a stack of insurance forms with plans to take them to the receptionist's desk for those in line who might possibly have some additional medical coverage, she turned and almost bumped into Jared. Her pulse, darn it, responded with a quick gallop. She'd remember that citrusy scent in the future, but only so he couldn't sneak up on her again.

He reached into his shirt pocket and pulled out a folded piece of paper. "I was in surgery all day yesterday, so I didn't have a chance to call you. Sorry, but I didn't think you'd appreciate a call after bedtime."

"How do you know my bedtime?"

The corner of his mouth twitched into a reserved smile. "I guessed."

She didn't smile back, refusing to look away. He didn't have a clue how important the test was to her, but why should he? It wasn't his problem. It was just some casual offer he'd made to give the illusion of being nice.

"Again, my apologies."

She saw something there, in his eyes, an earnest appeal? Give the guy a break, she told herself, it's only eight forty-five in the morning. She gave a quick nod.

"Anyway, here you go." He handed her the paper.

Forcing her gaze away, she unfolded it and found a date and time for a genetic marker study at a Massachusetts General hospital. She really needed to quit writing off people so quickly. "Thank you," she said, a little warm bubble rising in her chest. "I'll be there this Saturday."

"Good. Under ideal circumstances you could get the results in a week to ten days, but there's such a demand for this specialty they can't guarantee results that soon. Sorry."

"I understand." Her throat tightened at the thought of having the test done, and her pulse sped up, thinking about the potential results. With a shaky hand she took another sip of coffee. "How much will it cost, do you know?"

"It's all taken care of," he said.

"What do you mean?"

"Professional courtesy."

"Wait. What?"

"The lab extended the courtesy." He gave her a pointed look, and a little voice in the back of her head counseled her to shut up about it and be gracious. Though she didn't believe his explanation for a minute and really wanted to know who'd actually paid for the test, she nodded.

"Well, I guess we better get you signed into our computer system," she said, slipping the paper into her lab-coat pocket. "That line of patients is probably twice as long by now."

Ten minutes later they opened the doors and began processing the ever-expanding crowd. It appeared their little neighborhood had people crawling out of the crevices in need of care. Vincent acted as the triage nurse. Kasey saw the more general-needs patients, such as pap smears, breast exams, flu and vague complaints, and Jared took anyone who needed a surgical consult or onsite care.

Within an hour Jared approached her desk and asked for her assistance. She jotted down a few quick notes on the breast exam she'd just completed then gave him her complete attention.

"I've got a patient who came in for a cyst removal on his shoulder, which I've already done, but I want you to see this." She followed him into exam room two, where she saw a middle-aged man with a bright red complexion and one of his front teeth missing.

"This is Franklin O'Leary," Jared said. "Mr. O'Leary, this is Kasey McGowan, the nurse practitioner who runs this place, and I wanted to have her take a look at your stomach."

The man looked eight months pregnant with a rounded, bulging symmetrical contour. "If you don't mind," Kasey said, warming her hands while he lay flat on the examination table. "I'm going to do a little poking around."

"It's been a while since a lady's poked me anywhere. Go right ahead."

She smiled, then palpated the tightly distended skin and performed percussion, noting tympany over and around the navel, with dullness at his flanks.

"How long has your stomach been distended?" Jared asked.

"Dis—what?"

"Has your stomach been big like this for a while?" Kasey spoke up.

"A few months, I think. Just my beer gut."

Jared marked the level of dullness on the skin with a magic marker.

"Could use a new tattoo." The man glanced at the straight lines. "That's not what I had in mind, but what do you expect for free?"

Kasey smiled again, appreciating his New England humor.

"Lie on your side for a minute or so," Jared said, and waited for the patient to shift his position. The curly-headed man cooperated, though it was awkward to move with his big belly. Kasey helped him, hoping Jared would get the point.

As predicted, the dullness shifted. Kasey knew that meant textbook-wise there was at least five hundred cc of abdominal fluid and, judging from the size of the otherwise malnourished man's abdomen, she suspected a lot more.

"How much beer do you drink?" Jared asked.

"I'm known to have a pint or two whenever I can. Doesn't always work out, though."

Most people underestimated their drinking, and in Franklin's case the "whenever I can" could mean morning, noon and night.

"Roll on your back," Jared said, this time helping him. "Kasey, will you press here for me?"

She placed her hand firmly against the patient's abdomen in the navel area while Jared put the flat of his hand on the left side and tapped with his other hand. Sure enough, this generated a pressure wave indicating ascites.

"Do you have a history of cancer?"

"Not that I'm aware of, Doc. Should I get scared now?"

"I'm just asking questions. No need to worry." Jared gave her a decisive look. "We need to drain him," he said.

She nodded. Normally this procedure was done in an ER, but under the circumstances Franklin needed immediate medical attention. Suspecting he wouldn't follow through on his own if sent to the ER, and the cost of ordering an ambulance to transport him was off the budget, they'd go ahead and do what they could for him right here, right now.

"How would you like to lose a little weight and get your trim waist back?" Jared broached the subject.

"What do you mean?" Franklin said.

Jared explained, though in a rushed manner, that Franklin's liver wasn't functioning as it should, and how the fluid could be removed here in the clinic with an easy procedure, then it would be sent away to a laboratory for studies.

The man licked his lips and stared at the floor for a moment while he thought, then gave the okay. Jared's bedside manner could have been ten times better, but he didn't seem nearly as bad as she'd thought last week. He'd gotten Franklin to agree to an important test. The guy had arranged for the clinic and then shown up. Plus, he'd come through on the lab appointment for her. That said something about his character. A man of his word meant a lot to her these days, so she'd cut him some slack on his under-par bedside manner.

Kasey had Vincent bring in a consent form and she went hunting in the supply closet for an abdominal paracentesis kit. She asked Vincent to assist Dr. Finch, since the waiting room was packed with patients, and all the examination rooms were full.

She entered the next room and found a senior citizen with a swollen cheek and a nasty tooth abscess. In a perfect world this woman would go to her dentist, but from the look of her poorly cared-for teeth, she hadn't seen one in years. All Kasey could do was ask if she was allergic to any medicine and write her a prescription for generic antibiotics, point her to the local discount pharmacist and hope the patient followed her orders about taking the meds until they were finished, instead of stockpiling them for future use.

"Once the infection has calmed down a bit, you'll need to see a dentist."

"Ack, would rather have my cousin pull it."

Before lunch, Laurette Meranvil waited in room one to have her stitches removed. Jared tended to her and, as timing would have it, and admittedly because Kasey was curious, she ran into the patient on the way out. The laceration under Laurette's eye was a thin pink line.

The young woman smiled at Kasey.

"It's healing beautifully," Kasey said.

"I put special ointment from home on it."

"I may have to find out the name of your miracle ointment for our other patients."

"It's Haitian vetiver oil."

"Let me jot that down," Kasey said, making a note to Google it later. The woman walked with her head held high out the door, so different from last week when she'd come in covering her face.

Kasey took a moment to appreciate the much-needed help the clinic brought to the community. She glanced up and found Jared watching her. The usual tension had left his eyes, and she suspected he felt the same sense of pride she did, and wondered if he got that feeling doing cosmetic surgery. He nodded at her then slipped into the next exam room. Kasey might not be sure about the magical powers of Haitian vetiver oil, but she sure as heck knew there was some special voodoo in that man's stare.

And the day continued.

By late afternoon, Kasey couldn't keep track of how many patients she'd seen. Angie approached wearing her usual expression, as if she was in pain, brows knitted, world-weary. Kasey had gotten so used to the expression over the years she hardly took note.

"You've got to see this," Angie said. "It'll break your heart." At second glance, Angie did look more disturbed than usual, shaking her head, first clucking her tongue then pursing her lips.

Kasey followed the medical assistant into exam room three, where a mother and her toddler sat quietly. Angie was right, the pudgy little boy's cleft lip did break her heart. Did the mother think they could sew the lip together in the clinic and all would be well? She tried not to let her sadness show. The child probably had to endure sympathetic glances and an overabundance of pity every day. She didn't want to add to his pain or shame or whatever a two-year-old felt when people looked at him and treated him differently from everyone else.

"Hey, little fella," she said, with a big smile.

She fought an urge to pick him up and hug him tight, and tell him she had a magic pill that would make his sweet little mouth look like all the other children's. Then his big brown eyes would be the feature everyone first noticed, not his lip.

Offering her hand to the mother, Kasey maintained a professional manner. "What can we do for you today?"

The mother explained her son had been born with the problem, which, of course, Kasey already knew. He'd been born in another state, and the family couldn't afford surgery. They'd moved to Massachusetts partially because of the health insurance system. She examined the little boy's mouth and discovered that his palate was intact, and that the congenital deformity was limited to his lip. A good thing. Healthy and round, she realized he had no problem eating. She decided to let Jared take over on this consultation, and excused herself.

"Can you take a look at the toddler in room one?" she said, approaching Jared in the hallway and handing him the intake message. He glanced at Angie's notation then slowly back to Kasey. She hoped the boy's situation would touch his heart as much as it had hers.

"Sure," was all he said as he disappeared behind the exam-room door.

Kasey rubbed her eyes and took a moment to sit down and rest, wishing she had another cup of coffee for false energy.

Pressed for space, and between his triage duties, Vincent had set up a makeshift immunization station in the clean supply closet with no less than fifteen people standing patiently in line. She'd guess they'd seen over sixty patients already, and knew there were at least forty more waiting. At some point, if they wanted to get out of here before midnight, they'd have to cut off the line, and she really didn't want to be the person assigned to do that.

Angie brought another load of messages. Kasey picked the one off the top and before she headed for the next exam room noticed Jared come out from the other room and get on the phone. She overheard him talk to someone just before she entered the other exam room.

"I've got a little boy I'd like to refer for pro bono plastic surgery," he said, and her heart did a little extra pitty-pat of joy. The guy wasn't nearly as uncompassionate as he'd made himself out to be.

At some point, Vincent sent out for burgers and they ate on the run, having turned the day into a medical marathon. By ten o'clock the last patient left the clinic.

Exhausted yet exhilarated, Kasey grinned, hugged Vincent and high fived Angie. "We did it!"

"I think I'm numb," Vincent said.

"I died four hours ago," Angie said.

Jared stood quietly, as if taking in the scene. "You guys are a great team. I'm impressed. It's been an honor working with you."

"Same here, Doc," Vincent said, with a starry-eyed glance.

Kasey nodded and smiled, aware Jared hadn't thrown one single tantrum all day, like so many other doctors she'd worked with were inclined to do. No high drama. No added stress. Just noses to the grindstone, and their little community clinic had turned out to be one mean medical machine.

"Thanks for agreeing to my big idea," she said.

"You're welcome." His gaze met and held hers captive. She was the first to look away.

While Angie tidied up her desk and Vincent put his extra supplies away, Jared approached Kasey in the office. "There's only one thing I'm disappointed about today."

She cocked her head, furrowing her brow. What could he possibly be disappointed about? They'd seen a hundred and twenty-five patients! "You didn't get to see a gunshot wound? Oh, wait, let me guess, you were hoping for a stabbing."

He shook his head and smiled. "It's too late to take you out to dinner."

"Well, that's very kind of you, but I'd fall asleep in my salad if you did."

"So I was right about your bedtime, then."

"Don't get cocky on me, Doc." She grinned.

His gaze languished on her, and a tentative smile creased his lips. "Then we'll have to take a rain-check for when you're more alert."

"That's not necessary, Dr. Finch. Really."

"Jared," he said. "Call me Jared. Let's not take any steps backward, okay?" He took off his doctor's coat and put on his suede jacket, then gathered up his computer case and threw it over his shoulder. "You need a ride home?"

"Angie's dropping me off. Thanks, though."

"I could use a ride to the T," Vincent said, appearing at the door, his normally perfect hair limp and falling in his eyes.

"Sure," Jared said to Vincent, before he turned his attention back to Kasey. "I have the weekend with my kids, but name a day next week. I owe you dinner."

"Really, Jared, it isn't necessary."

He sat in front of her, took her hand, running his thumb over her knuckles. "Kasey, look at me."

She did and could barely take the effect of his solid blue gaze on her, let alone his touch. Spontaneous tingles popped up in unspeakable places.

"I want to. I really want to." He waited sufficiently long for his message to sink in, then released her hand and looked at Vincent. "Are you ready to go?"

Vincent nodded, jaw dropped over what had just transpired. Behind Jared's back, Vincent made eye contact with Kasey and gave her the thumbs-up sign. She wasn't sure if it was on his behalf for finagling a ride with the hot doc, or hers for getting that invitation for dinner. She shook her head. Jared really did feel sorry for her. She'd have to face the fact.

On his way to the door, Jared looked over his shoulder, another quick yet intense glance. It knocked Kasey in the chest like a mini fireworks blast, and left her staring at her desk, trying to catch her breath. Truth was he scared her.

She wondered what in the world "I want to. I really

want to." meant. Did the guy get off feeling sorry for sick girls or was he really interested in her? Yet how could he be considering what her future might hold? And why should she be interested in him other than because he was so damn gorgeous?

Since she was looking at a fifty-fifty chance in one area of her life, maybe she should start gambling with other aspects too. After all, to play it safe she'd come up with plan B—keep everything superficial. Don't get involved. Take what she could from each day, and enjoy it.

All the possibilities left her mind reeling, with an excited tickle under her skin, and a definite promise to herself to find out what Jared's true intentions were.

All she had to do was pick a day.

# CHAPTER FOUR

THE clinic felt like a ghost town the next morning, with only a handful of clients wandering in for various ailments. It was a good thing too, as Kasey was dragging from yesterday's manic pace. So were Vincent and Angie, Vincent being more quiet than usual and Angie with less of a scowl and making fewer snide remarks.

Later over lunch with Vincent in a hole-in-the-wall café three doors down, Kasey broached the topic still haunting her mind.

"V., can you go to an appointment with me on Saturday morning?"

"Are you finally getting highlights in your hair, and you want my guidance?" he said, eyes wide with excitement before taking a huge bite of his overstuffed sandwich.

Kasey loved his sense of humor and how he always managed to make her laugh, sometimes even when he wasn't trying to. "No, nerd ball, I've got a special test I need to take and I want you there with me."

All his attention settled on her face. "Is there something I should know?"

"I wanted to tell you on Friday night, but things got waylaid." Kasey gave him every single detail of her circumstances, noticing his eyes soften and well up by the time she'd finished. "So, I'd really like to have some back-up when I go for the test."

"Of course I'll be there, honey. Wouldn't miss it for the world. What time?" He got up, walked behind where she was sitting, leaned over and gave her a hug, his smooth cheek next to hers. He always smelled so good. "This Huntington's business is not going to happen to you. I won't let it. Do you hear me?"

Now she cried, too. She turned and they hugged closer. "Thanks, buddy."

"You bet."

Later, when they walked back to the clinic holding hands, she thought all a person really needed in the world was one good friend, and at the moment she held his hand tight.

Friday turned into another zoo day at the clinic, with patients arriving in groups. The weekend always brought in more folks—those warding off early illness, those making sure their pain medication would stretch through two more days, or those finally finding the time to get to the clinic about something that had been bothering them for weeks.

As the end of the day grew closer, Saturday's lab appointment loomed ahead, and a knot in the pit of Kasey's stomach wound tighter and tighter. She sat hunched over her desk, trying to convert pounds into kilograms and multiplying that by the dose of liquid antibiotics her pediatric patient in room four would need. Her brain as fuzzy as old cheese, she decided to use a calculator, and turned to walk to the cupboard.

Jared stood before her in faded jeans and a form-fitting pale blue sweater with the sleeves pushed up his forearms, which made his eyes so blue they were almost impossible to look at.

"What are you doing here?" she asked, just short of a gasp.

"I'm on my way out of town, decided to take a quick detour." He scratched his jaw. "Wanted to make sure everything was still a go for tomorrow."

"Yes. Vincent's going with me. I'll be at the lab in plenty of time." She forced a glance into his eyes, blinked and looked away as the nerve endings in her chest came alive. "Thanks again."

"Good." He didn't seem ready to leave, hands in his back pockets, glancing at his sports shoes and back at her. "You never got back to me."

Got back to him? She'd thought about him a dozen times since Tuesday. Remembering his almost-smile in between patients and how he'd gobbled down his burger on the run that night just like the rest of them. She'd used her index finger at the corner of her own mouth to let him know he'd had mustard there just before he'd entered a patient room. He'd gratefully licked it away while turning the doorknob, and she'd diverted her eyes because the sight of his tongue had thrown her for a loop. He'd gotten her the lab appointment, had said it was professional courtesy—to the tune of a thousand dollars: she'd researched the cost the next day—and offered her a ride home, and her impression of him had definitely changed for the better, but...

"You were supposed to tell me which day we can do dinner, remember?" His low and sexy voice rumbled through her already heightened nerve-endings, even if he was being pretty persistent.

The thought of Jared asking her to dinner had seemed so absurd that after he'd asked her she'd swept it to the back of her mind and tried to forget about it.

"Oh!" She leveled him with her stare. "You were just kidding, right?"

"Would I be here if I was kidding?"

By the look in his eyes, he wasn't fooling around. He wanted to take her to dinner and the thought of spending an entire evening with him, alone, made her palms tingle. After an awkward beginning, she'd survived Friday night at the bar and the coffee café with him, but this felt different. They'd broken the ice working side by side on Tuesday. He felt more familiar now, plus he knew her big secret.

She swallowed. "Well, in that case, Wednesday?"

"How about Monday? I just got scheduled for an evening Botox clinic on Wednesday that I have to participate in. And Tuesday is back to school night with the kids."

"Right." The thought of stone-faced Jared sticking needles into middle-aged women's faces for an entire evening brought some comic relief, though not nearly enough to help her relax.

Monday was so close. She'd need time to build up her defenses, to talk herself out of how gorgeous she found Jared, even if he was too darned serious and, when she thought about it, far too forward. She'd need time to ward off the self-consciousness of being an ordinary girl hanging out with a man who helped people look like movie stars. Every time he looked at her, the way he was doing right now, she wondered how far short of the mark she fell in his eyes.

He snapped his fingers. "So how about it?" he said.

She zipped out of her trance. "Dinner?"

"That's what I had in mind. Would you prefer dessert?" Something playful danced through his impatient gaze, sending her even more off balance.

She dropped her head. "Jared, I just don't get why—"

"I want to. Would you do me a favor and just say yes? Otherwise I'm gonna be late to get my kids." He looked at his watch.

Flustered and still off kilter, she laughed, and it helped. She unfisted her hand. "Okay. Sure. Thanks for asking. Wouldn't want to upset your ego." She half rolled her eyes, either an obvious sign of insecurity or a pure juvenile reaction, she wasn't sure which. The man had a way of mixing her up with a mere glance.

He approached and cupped her arm, giving it a squeeze. "Good luck tomorrow. I'll make you drink enough Monday night to forget all about waiting for the results. Deal?"

Frozen by the feel of his firm grasp, she found it hard to squeak out an answer. "Deal."

When she finally lifted her gaze, his look delved into her eyes, and more tiny zings of excitement zipped through her. This. Had. To stop.

He smiled. A real smile, not his usual tense excuse for one, and it was friendly, sexy and devious all at once. Way too devious. Kasey wasn't sure if her eyelids fluttered as his warmth rushed into her or if she drooled or what, because once again he'd stunned her to the spot.

"See you then," he said, letting go of her arm and walking off.

"Yeah, see you..." How the heck would she survive being around him if he dared look at her like that again?

On Saturday morning, Vincent sat in on the pre-test genetic counseling and Kasey was glad. Even though she'd studied genetics in science courses, her anxiety level kept her from taking in even one single sentence of information.

The clean, sterile-looking lab, with long white counters and stools, seemed more out of a movie set than a working lab. Behind swing doors with porthole windows she saw the functioning side of the department, with several people in white jackets bustling about, conducting various tests and other functions at their work stations.

After giving a speech about the autosomal dominant inheritance pattern, her fifty percent chance of inheriting it and drawing out a basic graph of stick figures indicating the four parent possibilities and the two child outcomes, the small, dried-apple-faced lab counselor, looked sympathetically through bifocals towards Kasey.

"We'll go ahead and make an appointment for you to see a neurologist, since it can take a few weeks to get a slot. In the meantime, I want you make a list to bring with you of any symptoms you may be experiencing, even if they don't seem related to the disease." He reached into his breast pocket. "Also, you can call this number to make an appointment with a therapist for extra support."

He handed her the business card, then several pieces of paper. "First, fill out this questionnaire, and then we'll draw the blood."

Vincent put his arm around her shoulder while she filled in her key personal information. He offered input when she balked at some of the questions.

"They want to know your recent life stress changes, so mention the main one—your father dropping this bombshell on you!"

"Oh, right," she said, her hand clammy and minutely trembling. She thought it might be due more to clutching the pen too tightly than early symptoms for Huntington's, yet she decided to include it on the questionnaire. *Hand tremors.* "Will you come with me to the neurologist appointment?"

"Of course!"

Having her best friend with her made the nerve-racking experience a bit more tolerable, but her heart thumped in her chest as if she'd taken the stairs instead of the elevator up all five floors. She'd grown up independent and strong, a conscious effort to be the exact opposite of her mother, yet under these circumstances she felt anything but confident.

After the paperwork, she was escorted to the blood draw table. Closing her eyes tight, she didn't watch when the lab tech tightened the tourniquet and took the blood sample. The only thing she could think about was how her entire future rested on this single vial of blood, and whether or not it contained a copy of the defective gene inherited from her father. A man she'd never even known. She hung and shook her head.

Light perspiration beaded above her lip, and the lab tech looked a little startled, as if she'd gone white or something. He reached into his pocket for an ammonia ampoule.

"I'm fine," she said, pulse pounding in her ears. "I didn't even feel the needle."

She took three deep breaths, clutched Vincent's hand, waited several seconds before she stood, then left the building, refusing to drag her feet, determined to enjoy the rest of her day. What was the alternative, go home and pull her bedcovers over her head?

With an appointment with a neurologist in one hand and a tentative follow-up lab appointment in one month to discuss the results in the other, and with Vincent by her side, she pushed through the large glass doors and out onto the loud and busy boulevard.

"Let's have lunch," she said, not feeling the least bit hungry. "My treat."

What her future would bring couldn't be stopped, and she wasn't really sure she wanted to find out, but she could make the rest of the day as pleasant as possible. It was, by far, her best option.

Just before closing on Monday night, Jared arrived at the community clinic through the back door looking gorgeous but distracted. His hair looked as if he'd run his fingers through it more than a few times. Kasey sat at her desk, typing the finishing touches on some nurse's notes. He approached with a grim, preoccupied expression instead of a friendly greeting.

"Are you ready?" he asked.

She swiveled around to face him head on. "You look sick or something. Are you sure you want to go through with this?"

With still no evidence of a smile, he sent a sharp look her way. "We made plans, I'm here, let's go."

Let's go? He sure knew how to make a girl feel special. "What makes you think I want to be stuck with a sourpuss like you for dinner?"

"We'll talk. Come on, grab your purse."

"No."

Surprised, as if he'd never been refused before, he lifted a brow and quit fiddling with his car keys. "No?"

She swiveled her chair back toward the desk. "You can't come in here with that attitude and expect me to jump at the chance of spending an hour with you."

"Two hours for dinner, at least." Her retort had bounced off his armor. "Now, come on, let's go."

"Not even five minutes. No way. I'm not a masochist." Secretly she'd been looking forward all day to seeing Jared tonight, but now she wasn't sure about spending the evening with him in this mood.

"I need to get out of here." He walked up to where she was sitting, took her wrist in his hand, turned and headed for the door. Refusing to stand, she let him pull the office chair on wheels a few feet across the floor. It felt silly, he looked ridiculous, and she needed to take charge or be humiliated. Was that his thing? To treat women like office furniture, to be moved at will, as he saw fit?

Rather than make an even bigger scene, since Vincent and Angie had already stopped what they were doing to watch, Kasey skidded her feet on the floor as brakes, stood, made a big deal about needing to grab her purse from her desk four feet away, and followed him. She'd put an end to their so-called date the minute they hit the street.

He glanced over his shoulder, this time with a grateful look, and there it was, the hint of pain in his eyes. She'd seen it the very first day they'd met, and again at the bar when he'd mentioned his kids. Obviously something was going on, and he wasn't capable of talking about it right now. A twinge of compassion, though against her better judgment, changed her decision to stick it out with him.

"See you guys tomorrow," she said as he tugged her impatiently towards the door.

"Have fun, kids," Vincent said, in an obvious attempt to lighten the atmosphere.

"Yeah, don't do anything I wouldn't do," Angie said in her monotone voice and with the usual pained expression.

Jared ignored both of them.

"Will do," Kasey said, tossing them a perplexed glance.

When they got to the car, Jared glanced at her feet. "Are those shoes okay for walking?"

"Yes. I've walked in them all day."

"Good, because if you don't mind, I'd like to walk awhile before we eat."

"How far are we walking?"

"I'm not sure. I'll know when I start to feel better."

"What's on your mind, Jared?" He opened the passenger door for her. "I thought we were walking?"

"Not here, once we get there."

"Where's there?" She jutted out her hip and placed her hand on it. "You're confusing the heck out of me."

"Where we're having dinner."

He hadn't made eye contact since he'd first arrived and still looked agitated as all hell. Something big was going on. More confused than ever, she got into his nondescript sedan, the questions building with each second.

"We'll talk later," he said, leaning in before shutting the door.

Tension seemed to rise off him like a heat wave over asphalt. She was quite sure it had nothing to do with her, so she sat back and rested her head on the upholstery. Until he was ready to talk, there was no way she'd get anything out of him. But, really, did she need this stress on top of her own problems?

Once he was inside the car, she pinned him with her stare and a surprise attack. "You owe me a lobster dinner for this, buddy."

One corner of his mouth twitched. Zing, she'd chinked his armor. "How about a lobster roll? I'm on a budget."

She shook her head and smiled, grateful he was loosening up. "Whatever."

With that he started the car and headed south on Route 99, the second movement of Beethoven's Seventh Symphony on his CD player perfectly matching his overly dramatic mood. Hmm, she hadn't pegged him as a classical music guy. She glanced around and noticed evidence of his kids in the car with a discarded takeaway bag under her feet and a bag of half-eaten chips left on the dashboard. At least he wasn't obsessive-compulsive clean, like so many other surgeons she'd known.

A little over twenty minutes later they parked in the hospital doctors' lot. Once again without a word, he grabbed her hand, and they walked a few blocks until they hit the meandering Charles River Path from north station Causeway, by Paul Revere Park and the USS Constitution Museum.

"Are you jogging or do you call this walking?" Kasey said, trying to keep up with Jared's determined stride, the constant feel of his hand heating up her arm. It was drizzling and she wished she'd brought her umbrella. He didn't seem to care.

"Sorry," he said, deep in thought, as he slowed down the slightest bit, not letting go of her but pulling her along.

The brisk evening air gave Kasey new energy, but she wasn't ready to run a mile for her dinner. The distraction of being palm to palm with him grew harder to ignore with each step. "So where're we going?"

"The Tavern on the Water."

She'd heard of it, but had never been there. "Good food?"

"Good view. And they've got lobster rolls."

"Better be good." She was out of breath. "You ready to talk yet?"

"Nope." He picked up the pace, and she promised herself not to bring up his talking again unless she felt like breaking into a sprint.

Ten minutes later they arrived at a two-story boathouse with a superb view of the harbor. Due to the drizzle, which hadn't let up and had most assuredly left her hair frizzy and a mess, they headed straight upstairs and inside.

The place was crowded with young professionals from the nearby schools, businesses, and medical facilities. Jared nearly had to elbow his way to the bar.

"Two beers." He named his favorite brand and the pale ale she'd been drinking the other night. Interesting, he'd remembered.

He handed her the bottle and led her to a tall table in the corner that had just opened up.

After she got settled, took a sip of her beer, and sized up Jared's supersized foul mood, she decided to read the menu rather than provoke him with more questions. The cozy harbor view calmed her, and after the energetic walk she was more than ready to eat, even if the company was the worst she'd been around in ages. Actually, not so. She remembered a spectacularly horrible date a couple months back. At least Jared was pretty to look at. Maybe he wasn't so bad after all.

Jared took a long slow draw on his beer. He must have come straight from work because he wore dark slacks and a sports coat and a lilac-colored shirt, accenting his eyes. But then again, what didn't? She noticed how his lashes were so thick they separated into clumps, then she looked quickly away at some ultrachic apartments right on the waterfront.

After another swallow or two Kasey saw the bunched muscle at the corner of Jared's jaw twitch, then give up as if worn out. He stared hard at the pewter-colored water. All the happy little party lights blinking along the window-frame couldn't change his mood. She knew better than to think she could either. After several drawn-out sighs and another drink of beer, he placed the bottle on the table between his hands and worked at turning it round and round while peeling at the label.

"So, my kids told me they're going to Europe for a month this summer." He tore a big chunk off the label for emphasis. "Four flipping weeks."

He stared at Kasey with furious eyes, and an old saying came to mind: *If looks could kill.* Hey, buddy, I didn't do it!

"Would have been nice to know, as I was planning a camping trip in New Hampshire with them before school started up again." He looked like a man ready to punch a wall. "And here's the real kicker, they miss their friends back home and want to move back to California. Patrice has already found a new school for them, this one's in Malibu. They'll start in the fall."

Kasey noticed he had several scratches across the slightly swollen knuckles of his right hand, and wondered if he'd already punched something.

He was a surgeon. He wouldn't risk hurting his hands...would he? But his ex was playing games with him, even she could see that.

"She knows I'm committed here for another year, and she didn't even consult me on it."

Kasey knew better than to say a word. Her job would be to listen tonight, and seeing Jared's tortured gaze, knowing how much his kids meant to him, she changed her perspective, suddenly willing to listen for as long as it took.

"It's so frustrating to be left out of the loop about something this important, as if I don't count." His gaze lifted to meet hers. "I'm their father, dammit. I'm not going to just give up and go away."

"I think that's great. The world needs more fathers like you."

Her words softened his glare. "Thank you." He looked downright grateful and definitely more hand-some when he didn't scowl. He reached for her forearm, his long fingers lightly caressing her skin before they slid south and patted her hand then retreated to his side of the table. "I needed to hear that."

"I meant it. You obviously care a great deal about your kids." She gazed at him long enough to connect with his intense eyes, which sent a tiny shiver through her.

As far as first dates went, this one was a doozy, but how could she be mad at a man so hungry to be involved with his children? Wouldn't she have given anything in the world to know her father when she was a kid? She glanced up and caught him staring at her. He didn't look like he was thinking about his children just then.

If a man could be this passionate about his children, could he be the same about a woman? His touch had heated her skin, and the guy wasn't even trying to come on to her.

Kasey needed another sip of beer to ward off the threatening and highly inappropriate warmth starting in an unmentionable part of her body. That brisk walk had really gotten her blood flowing and right now it had pooled in a spot she shouldn't even be thinking about.

"Patrick has been telling me he misses his soccer

buddies back home, and Chloe texts her best friend back in California every day, but I thought they were okay with this school, and I'm here. Doesn't that count for something?"

"That's what frequent flyer programs are for," she said. "And red-eyes."

He screwed up his face. "Come again?"

"Be the game changer in your relationship with your kids. Be there for them no matter what. You'll just have to fly back to California every other weekend to see the kids. Let them know you will *always* be in their lives, no matter where they live."

The corner of his mouth twitched, tension left his eyes, his brows smoothed. "Good point. I won't take this lying down."

Hearing him say the words *lying down* planted another improper thought in her head. What was her problem?

Meanwhile, he continued to talk and, though she'd temporarily tuned out, she studied him carefully. His dark lashes curtained incredible eyes. The nostrils of his straight nose microscopically flared with emotion while he continued to pour out his heart. Only hearing a word here and there, she watched, thinking inappropriate thoughts. Back at the office he'd been pushy, but now these words about his family came straight from his heart. It touched her in a way that took her by surprise, and, shameful as it was, turned her on.

The guy needed to let off some steam or his head would burst. These days, she could relate to that feeling. Heck, she needed to let off some steam, too. Though she couldn't possibly know his reasons for asking her to dinner, she liked this wicked physical response he drew out of her without even trying. What magic could he spin if he tried?

He'd kept her preoccupied, and she liked it that she hadn't lost a single second to her own worries so far tonight.

Yeah, she'd cut Jared some slack, let him talk all he wanted. Not only because he made her feel horny but because she really wanted him not to hurt so much. Besides, if history really did repeat itself, after tonight she'd probably never see the dude again anyway. So tonight she'd be a team player, help him forget about his worries.

And later, as superficial as it sounded, maybe she'd get lucky.

# CHAPTER FIVE

WHAT in the hell was Jared doing, spilling his secrets to a woman he hardly knew? Kasey sat across the table squirming with discomfort and yet he couldn't shut up. Could he help it if she was easy to talk to? Every date guru in the world warned against talking about your last relationship with the new. Relationship? Was that what this was about? He'd only met her a week ago.

And yet. No. Absolutely not. He wasn't in the market for a relationship. It took too much effort, and his ex had cured him of believing in love. From now on he'd keep life uninvolved and uncomplicated where women were concerned.

"Maybe you can take the kids camping at the beginning of summer? You know, before they go to Europe?" She picked up her overflowing-with-lobster roll and took a vigorous bite. Why did he find that sexy? Damn, he needed to get out more.

"I have no choice," he said, digging into his own lobster roll, "but I'll do it, even if it means changing my plans."

"Cuz…love…kids. You…gud fah-fer." It sounded muffled by food, but he got the gist of what she'd said.

He sighed, and chewed without interest in taste or texture. He'd spent enough time working himself up over a situation he couldn't change. He needed to let it go, give himself a break. Hell, he sat across from a young and vibrant woman, a fresh natural breath of air from what he'd dealt with all day. Tonight she seemed to be the game-changer. His eyes were drawn to the neckline of her loose-weave summer sweater, and the pale silver camisole beneath—not a hint of breast on view, yet the fit promised natural curves and fascinated the heck out of him.

It occurred to him how twisted his mind had become. He'd spent the day looking at women's breasts both pre—and post-surgery, and hadn't had one single sexual thought. Quite the contrary. He'd been all business. Yet Kasey, taking a great big bite of lobster roll and wearing a conservatively cut sweater, managed to stir up some purely prurient thoughts. He took it as a healthy breakthrough then wondered what she'd look like with her hair loose and tousled after a night in bed.

Was that the real reason he'd pushed for dinner tonight? Disappointment stopped him in mid-bite. He'd been concerned enough about Kasey to arrange for the genetic testing, genuinely concerned, and worried what her outcome might be, too. More than anything, he was surprised that he had a shred of empathy for anyone these days. She'd come out of nowhere and blindsided him.

He knew she needed a friend. Yet tonight he'd selfishly used her because she was a nurse and a good listener.

Right now, watching her eat, well, his wandering thoughts were anything but appropriate. Again, she'd blindsided him, and he needed to rein himself in.

Kasey lifted her gaze and unselfconsciously gave a bulging, closed-mouthed smile. She covered her mouth with the napkin, those mischievous green eyes peering over the top. "This is delicious."

"I'm glad." He smiled, thinking she was delicious, too. Delicious to look at. He went back to eating, all stirred up. Though feeling guilty about them, he liked the stirred-up feelings. Welcomed them. Great. Just what he needed, more confusion in his life. "For putting up with me, you deserve some dessert."

She smiled, and over the course of dinner he'd looked forward to each smile she shared. "Only if you'll share it with me."

An hour later, uncomfortably full from the chocolate molten cake, and as it had quit drizzling, he suggested they walk a bit more.

"If we stroll, count me in," she said, "but I'm through jogging." Again, she lanced him with those mischievous eyes.

He smiled, enjoying how she always sparked a reaction. "Okay." Realizing his mood had shifted from sour to spicy over the course of the meal, he wasn't ready to call it a night. Not nearly.

This time she beat him to it. She grabbed his hand and, though surprised, he twined his fingers through hers, completely aware of the connection and the hot path winding through his body.

He looked into her gaze. It wasn't his imagination. He saw the dark spark in her eyes, too. "I've been very selfish tonight."

She cocked her head. "You think?"

"I apologize."

"Don't worry about it."

Her easygoing manner enchanted him, but the fit of her sweater and curve of her slacks moved him far beyond enchantment. Hell, where was his head tonight?

The woman was literally waiting for a potential death sentence. A brutally cruel curse of a disease that would alter the course of her life, and he'd griped about not getting his fair share of parenting time through most of dinner. He ought to be dragged into the bay and dunked. But he could fix things. She'd given him several suggestions, too.

Maybe he could help Kasey open up and talk about her fears. He didn't want her to keep things tucked inside on his behalf. She deserved the same freedom he felt with her.

Had some empathetic person snuck in and inhabited his body? This wasn't his style at all, yet...

"Are you going to seek counseling?" he said. "I've heard..."

Kasey stepped in front of him, cupped his jaw with both hands and pulled him closer. "I don't want to talk about anything else tonight," she said, just before planting her mouth on his.

Stopped in his tracks, and not the least bit interested in arguing the point, he kissed her back. Her sweetly padded lips were smooth and warm and she moved them over his with vigor. Wanting more control, he scooped her waist close with one hand and cupped the back of her neck with the other, then shifted his head for a deeper kiss, a slick, silky kiss. She tasted sweet, like chocolate syrup, and his mind scrolled through thoughts of licking that syrup off a thousand different parts of her body. He groaned.

Her hands were now in his hair, and he held her so close his belt buckle pushed into his skin. The soft press of her breasts on his chest was his undoing. His fingertips skimmed from hip to waist to side, stopping at her breast, lifting and pressing the plump softness. He couldn't resist taking her breast into his hand, stroking his thumb over the nipple. This time he was positive the groan came from her side of the embrace.

As their mouths kissed and devoured and plunged, he became aware of two things—her hands had found their way under his shirt, working wonders on his skin, and he had a full, throbbing erection.

Good thing it was dark out.

They broke for air, and her panting breath turned him on even more, if that was possible. Forehead to forehead, he nosed down her cheek then nibbled her ear. Everything he did got a reaction out of her, making the situation below his belt more unbearable. He didn't want to stop, but they were in public, and a nurse and a doctor, well. Weren't they supposed to be practical about such things?

Her hand discovered his bulge, she gently squeezed, and since he couldn't think any more, he moved in for more kisses and full body presses.

The wake of a distant motorboat lapped a bucket worth of water over the harbor deck, and their feet were suddenly drenched.

Jared and Kasey gasped in unison.

Jared had never driven so recklessly in his life. Kasey gave him directions for the back route, and called out the turns. *Left here. Take your next right. Yield to the right. See that brick building? Turn left there. No. There.* He wondered if she'd be a bossy lover, and marveled over the fact he was pretty damn sure he was about to find out, and might even like it.

They made it to her home in less than twenty minutes, though they had to drive around the block once to backtrack for parking on her one-way street.

Still completely turned on, Jared watched as Kasey fiddled with her keys at the side of the house, before bursting through the door. Burning to touch her again, he grabbed her and waltzed her against the kitchen counter for another kiss.

"Wait!" She pushed him away. "I've got to turn off the alarm." He was so focused, he hadn't even heard it.

In a heartbeat she'd done the task, then grabbed him by the hand and tugged him through the kitchen down a short hallway to her bedroom.

The unmade bed looked completely inviting. He'd singlehandedly unbuttoned his shirt and slid out of half of it before he'd even hit the room. Her neck and ears were still red from their makeout session by the harbor, and the hold-onto-your-hats ride home hadn't lessened the sexy sparkle in her eyes.

She pulled the loose-knit sweater and cami over her head and he sucked in his breath at the sight of her lacy-bra-covered breasts. She was deliciously curvy, and he couldn't wait to hold and feel her again. Now both half-undressed, they came together in a tight embrace. He savored her warmth and smooth skin, the impact of her body so close to his, and his hands skated over her, searching for the bra clasp. On the way, he got distracted kissing the curve of her shoulder and just below her ear, and was rewarded with another deep sigh and shiver. Kasey seemed completely in tune with him, every touch and each kiss emitting uninhibited reactions, which turned him on more and more. He removed her bra and felt the heat and weight of her breasts in his palms, wanting nothing more than to bury his face in them. Her pebbled, rosy-pink nipples called out to be kissed. He wanted to do everything at once, all while being buried inside her.

They needed to get completely naked. Fast!

Kasey kicked off her shoes and shimmied out of her slacks and underpants while Jared did the same. God, he was sexy. Not an ounce of excess flesh anywhere, natural muscles rippled and flinched with each move. And, man, oh, man, was he ready for her.

*Not thinking. Not thinking. Keep it superficial.*

She shooed Miss Daisy off the bed and received a serious warning glance and meow. "Sorry, sweetie." Her cat had gotten used to being the center of her attention, and as Kasey dove on top of Jared, already reclined on the bed and reaching out for her, the cat got the point and took off.

Jared's smooth, hot skin was reward enough, but the hooded, dark-sea stare nearly made her crumple at his feet. *I am not worthy but, boy, am I glad he's here.*

His hands with long surgeon's fingers welcomed every part of her body, soon finding two favorite spots, her right butt cheek and left breast, where his mouth did amazing things. She'd been wet and ready since their world-class kiss in Charlestown, so she straddled his hips and, sweet heaven on earth, he adjusted himself, pressing against and sliding over the pick-me-first nub outside. Several moments passed, doing this heady teasing dance, his erection nudging and massaging her, his hands exploring her breasts, heightening her desire, tension twining ever tighter in her core. Being above and in charge, though feeling completely out of control, she widened her thighs, hoping he'd slide inside.

As though getting a sudden slap in the face, common sense reared its frustrating head. "Wait."

Jared came out of his trance, but barely.

"Condom," she breathed, her breasts skimming his chin when he lifted his head, his eyes looking on fire.

Jared dropped his head on the pillow with a thud and let out a frustrated moan.

"What? No just-in-case-I-get-lucky wrapper in your wallet?"

He shook his head, his lustful look quickly dissolving into disappointment. So he really wasn't a Casanova. Good. "You didn't plan this?"

"I just wanted someone to gripe to tonight, and you were it. Didn't expect you to be so sexy about it."

He was a gentleman after all, hadn't come prepared, hadn't planned on screwing her. The thought turned her on even more.

"Good thing one of us is prepared, then," she said pertly as she reached across the bed for the drawer. She'd been off the dating market for a while, but still probably had some condoms. Somewhere. She sure hoped so, anyway, and if she was lucky, they wouldn't be outdated.

While Kasey balanced on one knee and hand to reach across the bed and pull out the drawer with the other, Jared scooted down and shocked her with a deep kiss and nibble. A reward? Just as she grabbed the condom, when he included his tongue along with another kiss at her entrance, all thoughts left her head, instead pooling between her legs where Jared sent deliciously warm shockwaves throughout her body.

She didn't move and he didn't stop.

A few minutes later, crumpled by her orgasm but determined to stay on top, she sheathed him and guided him inside, and his groan of pleasure matched hers. Looking down into his sex-darkened eyes, his hands moving her hips over his heat and strength, seeing the blissful satisfaction on his face, she powered on as a second release rolled through her.

* * *

*Where has this gorgeous, sexy woman been all my life?*
Unable to hold back another second, Jared rolled Kasey
onto her back and lifted her hips to meet his quicken-
ing thrusts. Her body melted into his. He hadn't spent
nearly enough time marveling in it, but it was too late
now, they'd moved way past getting acquainted. He'd
take it slower next time.

Hard and harder he took her. Every last bit of energy
in his body focused on their connection, the sheer perfection of it. Her heat and tight feel. Her total response
to him as he realized she'd come again. Her quivering
over and around his erection as he drove deeper. The
power and intensity sent him over the edge, releasing
a mega-force of staggering pleasure, completely losing
himself to the sky dive.

Kasey woke to a quiet room, two eyes staring at her.
Miss Daisy. Miffed from inattention. She sat up. The
other side of the bed was empty. She should have known
better than to expect to see Jared there. They'd given in
to desire. Lust. Pure and simple. He'd made love to her
twice, the first crazy, like scratching an itch, the second much slower and even more amazing. Wow. She'd
lost count of her orgasms.

She sat at the side of the bed. No, she wouldn't let
self-doubt sneak in. This was her plan B. Superficial,
uncomplicated sex. They were adults and had done exactly what they'd wanted to do. That was all.

She walked to the kitchen to make some coffee and
feed the cat. Her body felt alive and maybe a little achy
but, wow, she liked feeling this way. He'd kept her so
busy and content she hadn't had a single second to
worry about her future. And she'd slept like a rock.

"Maybe I can sign him up for the next month until I

get my results, huh, Daisy?" The cat rubbed her ankle and walked between her legs.

"I'll probably never see him again, you know." She stood straighter, squaring her shoulders before stooping to feed the cat. "I don't need to. What's the point?" She scratched the cat's ears while Daisy ate.

A small piece of paper caught her eye on the kitchen table. *Had an early surgery. Thanks for last night.*

Although there was no mention of calling her, at least it was something. They'd had dinner, then sex. He'd left a note. This was the protocol for a no-strings kind of fling, just what she needed.

Kasey would put on her armor and deal with the consequences of having wildly hot sex with Dr Tall, Dark and Gorgeous, like a grown-up.

She'd done it. It was fantastic. Now it was time to forget him and move on before she invested any feelings in him. There was just one flaw to that logic. It wasn't her style, and she already had.

# CHAPTER SIX

WEDNESDAY afternoon at the clinic, with not a single word from Jared since Monday night, Kasey went through a stack of lab results. Franklin O'Leary's lab studies were back, and it wasn't good news. They'd found cancer cells in the paracentesis fluid and he would need further studies, possibly hospitalization, to help discern the primary source of cancer.

Kasey scrolled through the makeshift file she had for him, and found his cellphone number.

She'd tried her best to put Jared out of her mind since Monday night, deciding he was nothing more than a one-hit wonder. Wonder being the perfect word to describe what she'd experienced when making love with him. Now, with the discovery of cancer cells in Franklin's ascites, she felt compelled to tell Jared.

A hard lump formed in the pit of her stomach, followed by a queasy wave. Consequences. Damn it all, she'd acted exactly like her mother, and now had to face the consequences. She'd had sex with a man she hardly knew, a fellow professional, and though they didn't officially work together, she'd crossed the line on her personal rule. Now she'd still have to follow up with Jared on a strictly business level. It wouldn't be easy, but she needed to give him Franklin O'Leary's lab report.

She scrubbed her hands over her face, took a deep breath, and dialed his cellphone number. After four rings, it went to voicemail. Deciding to ignore the phony chirpy social voice, she kept her message all business, gave him the results and asked how he'd like to follow up.

With cancer cells floating around in abdominal fluid, which meant metastases, Mr. O'Leary needed to be seen immediately. She'd give Jared an hour to get back to her then she'd contact Franklin herself and ask him to come in to the community clinic as soon as possible. If necessary, she could request hospital admission for him.

The next chart to cross her desk made her sit up straighter. Bat bite? Did the city of Everett even have bats? Wondering what waited in room number three, she headed down the hall.

A young girl sat sullenly on the examination table, her mother standing next to her wearing a worried expression, biting her lips, fear apparent in the form of constricted pupils.

After introductions, Kasey asked the mother to get right to the story.

"Tessa has nightmares about once a week, and last night she ran down the hall telling me a bird was in her room and it woke her up when it bit her. My husband checked it out and couldn't find anything, but this morning I found this on her."

The mother lifted the six-year-old's long, brown hair to show two tiny pin prick marks on her shoulder. Kasey paused as a rush of possibilities scrolled through her head. The marks didn't look like a scratch, or any spider bite she'd ever seen, unless it was one huge spider.

"Do you own a kitten or puppy?"

The woman shook her head.

"And your husband didn't find anything in Tessa's room?"

She shook her head again. "He turned on the lights and did a quick sweep of her room. I've kept the door closed and haven't gone back in because I think there's a bat in there." Tears welled in the young mother's eyes and the child, picking up on her mother's distress, got restless.

"I want to go. Can we go now?"

"In a minute, honey," the mother said.

"What makes you think it's a bat?" Kasey asked.

"I've read about bats being able to bite people without them feeling it." She scratched her neck, with nervous, quick-moving fingers and whispered, "I'm worried about rabies." She creased her lips tightly to hold back the fear mounting in her eyes.

What the heck was *she* supposed to do? She needed to research bat bites before she could give an educated answer or allay this woman's fears. Only one thought prompted her to answer—what if she was a mother and this was her child?

"Though it is possible, it is highly unlikely that this is a bat bite. And even if it is a bat bite, the odds of that bat having rabies are low. I'd have to look up the incidence of rabies in our bat populations."

"What's rabies?" Tessa asked.

Oh, gosh, Kasey had forgotten how attuned young children were to adult conversations. She'd blown it, and wanted to kick herself for potentially scaring the little girl. "It's like an infection, and if a person has it they need to have medicine to treat it."

Tears, like small waterfalls, splashed over the mother's lower lids. Kasey was treating two patients, one who needed to calm down. But could she blame the mother? Fear of the unknown could start as a spark and spread to a flash fire if not handled properly.

"Like the pink stuff I take sometimes?"

"This medicine is different, but maybe you won't have to take it," Kasey said.

That seemed to satisfy the little one's curiosity.

"Well, here's what I recommend we do. First I'll wash this area for several minutes. Did you wash it with soap and water last night?" The mother nodded. "Good. Is Tessa up to date on her immunizations? Tetanus?"

The mother nodded again.

"Good." Kasey fished through the cabinets for a surgical sponge that already had antiseptic soap infused in it. She popped open the plastic and got it wet then began scrubbing the little girl's shoulder. "Does this hurt?" Tessa shook her head. "Since you haven't opened the bedroom door since last night, maybe you can have a pest-control person come and search the room for evidence of a bat?"

"I'll do whatever you say I should," the mother said.

When Kasey finished up the wash and left tincture of iodine over the two tiny marks they'd agreed as the course of action. Kasey gave Tessa a cherry lollypop and some stickers, though worry made the young one's eyes look even bigger. On the way out, as the child ran ahead, the mother grabbed Kasey's arm. "What if it is a bat bite, and we find it and it does have rabies?"

"We'd have to begin rabies post-exposure prophylaxis within ten days. Don't panic yet. We don't even know if this is a possibility. Please try to stay calm. I know it's hard."

The woman's clutch on Kasey's arm let up. "We've only got ten days to figure this out?"

Kasey gave a solemn nod.

After they left, Kasey didn't know if the mother was delusional or on top of a rare but conceivable possibility. Since the clinic was slow this afternoon, she went directly to her desk and computer to do some research, soon getting lost in the project and losing track of time. At least these days the treatment wasn't as bad as in the past. No more multiple painful injections into the abdomen. These days it would be like receiving a flu shot, five different times over four weeks, along with an initial intradermal immune globulin close to the actual site of the bite.

A shadow darkened her computer screen. Assuming it was Vincent being snoopy, she turned in her swivel chair, ready with a smart-aleck remark. But there stood Jared, dark brown polo shirt, piercing blue eyes, as handsome as ever. All thoughts left her head. The adrenaline pop in her chest couldn't be ignored. She chose irritation as her cover.

"Do you *not* know how to call first?"

"What would be the fun of that?" A slow, sexy smile stretched across his face and she thought she might turn to a puddle of drool right before his eyes, so she kept up her tough-chick act.

"Seriously. You've got to quit showing up out of the blue."

He rolled over Vincent's swivel chair, turned it backwards and threw his leg over like a cowboy mounting a horse. Crossing his elbows over the back, he continued to smile, undaunted by her hardball façade.

"You called. I'm here."

"Don't you have some Botox clinic tonight or something?"

"I asked a first-year fellow to take over." He reached out and touched her shoulder, sending another titillating message in the form of tiny feathers tickling flesh and nerve endings. "So let's see those lab results."

After fishing around her desk for the printed-out labs, she found them and handed them to him. "You'll never guess what I saw today," she said.

"The elephant man?"

She screwed up her face and shook her head. "Where do you get your ideas?"

He shrugged. "You told me to guess."

"You're weird. Never mind. I saw a little girl with a potential bat bite."

"Get out of town!"

"Really. I hope her mother is wrong."

"Me too," he said, now seriously studying the lab results. "Did you call Franklin O'Leary?"

"I was waiting to hear from you." She picked up the phone and dialed, with little hope of actually reaching the patient. Surprise, surprise, he picked up on the first ring.

Kasey gave Franklin the lowdown about his lab reports being back and asked if he could come to the clinic to talk about them. More surprise, he said he'd be right over.

"I was going to come pay you a visit anyway, Ms. McGowan, because my tummy's getting big again, and I'm feeling a bit weird today."

"That's definitely a good reason to come right away, Franklin. We'll see you as soon as you can get here."

After reading the labs, Jared's expression changed. "We need to admit him to the hospital."

"Agreed."

"We'll talk to Mr. O'Leary first, then I'll call in my admission report."

"Vincent can help you with anything you need."

Jared reached over the chair and lightly traced Kasey's jaw with his fingertips. "I don't think he can help me with *everything* I need."

Okay, he'd stopped her cold again, had her at hello, as the movie went. How was she supposed to respond? She wanted to ask why he hadn't called her, but that hardly qualified for relationship-lite status. Besides, she'd turned over a new leaf, hadn't she? Since she had a potential health crisis hanging over her head, the answer to which she wouldn't know for sure for a couple of weeks, shouldn't she live one day at a time and just go for it? Knock him on/off balance by being the no-strings-attached bedroom pal of his dreams?

What about the pep talk that morning? She'd already let her guard down, and some feelings had seeped in for Jared. It wasn't safe to play no-strings starting out with a handicap. But he was there, looking sexy as hell, making all the right moves and saying all the right things.

Damn, she was easy.

She swallowed against a suddenly dry throat, feeling completely out of character from her usual practical and cautious self. "Any time. You name the place." She was quite sure a mischievous gaze accompanied her parry.

After a small but obvious burst of something in his eyes—surprise or turn-on, she wasn't sure which—he glanced around the office with a purposeful gaze.

"Hold on, not here, cowboy," she lifted her hands, steadying the nervous boost.

He lifted his brows and cocked his head. "Was worth a shot."

There was that wicked sexy smile again. The game was on. She shook her head, feigning disgust.

In one week he'd morphed from a standoffish merely obligated surgeon into the sexiest thing she'd seen in a white coat in her entire life. Huntington's be damned, she was going for it, living in the solid present and not going to bother to look back...or forward. At least, not yet.

"Maybe we should lay down some rules with this thing..." she gestured with her hand back and forth between them "...we've got going."

"Such as?"

"No showing up out of the blue."

"What's the fun in that?"

"Okay," she said. "How about you don't have to feel obligated to call me the next day."

"Unless I want to?"

"Unless you want to."

"On this list of rules of yours, is there a limit on how often I can see you?"

"That's a good question."

"Did I tell you I hate lists?"

"We can skip the list, but I feel like we need some ground rules."

"I've lived by ground rules my entire life," he said. "Just once I'd like to wing it."

"You mean, just see how it goes?"

"A novel idea. Let's do that."

"I don't know how that works."

"I don't either, but I like the way it sounds." He grilled her with his dark look. "It sounds sexy. Exciting. Just like you."

If looks could kill, then looks could also make a woman turned on to the point of squirming in her swivel chair. She refused to be the first to look away. Her throat went parchment dry.

Jared unwrapped his leg from the chair, and instead of stealing a kiss he walked across the office to the

water cooler. Such a tease. He wasn't the only one needing a cold drink.

Vincent finally discovered him and started a conversation. Shaken by their attempt and subsequent fail-
ure to figure out how to handle what apparently was a
budding hot-to-the-point-of-nuclear-fusion affair, she
rushed back into safe territory, to the bat research.

Kasey looked great in her bright pink scrubs. He
even liked the matching clogs and socks with tiny pink
hearts around the rim. Not at all the kind of outfit he'd
expect a wild and sexy bedroom buddy to wear. How
could they put rules on this thing between them? First
they'd have to figure out what it was, and he feared if
they did that, the label would ruin all the fun. Couldn't
they just go with it? Figure things out as they went
along? The thought was as new and refreshing as the
cooler water.

Jared covertly watched Kasey at her computer while
chatting with Vincent near the water cooler. Her hair
was parted on the side and pulled up into a loose bun
with plenty of straggling strands to make him want to
twist them around his finger and pull her close for a
kiss. It was the first thought he'd had when he'd seen
her today and a continuing image now.

What the hell had he been doing, acting all smooth
earlier, as if ready to play a wolf and sex kitten game?
Was he ready to pull off an affair? Totally out of character, he admitted he liked the break from his usual
responsibilities and cares, and he definitely liked spending down time with Kasey. A quick flash of her naked
and on top of him made him refill his paper water cup
and take a huge gulp. What was Vincent talking about?
Now was not the time or place to give in to a rapidly
building desire for her, and the feeling was no doubt the

other L word—nothing more than unadulterated lust. Yeah, that was the angle he'd take this time around.

He hadn't called her since Monday because he didn't want to come on too strong, yet that was exactly what he'd just been doing. Vincent was telling him something, but he didn't have a clue what it was.

He had never had an affair when he'd been married, that wasn't part of his honor code, and if he was going to start one now, maybe they should keep to the rules. Yet he'd teased and played with her when she'd tried to make up a rule or two just now. Damn, he was out of his element. All he knew for sure was he wanted what happened Monday night to happen again. And soon. Maybe he should make that rule number one.

"These are all of the admission papers you'll need to fill out for the hospital," Vincent said. "We can do a quick physical here first."

"Sure thing." Jared reminded himself he'd come here for business, but after work he'd give himself permission to enjoy life a little.

As if she knew he was thinking about her, Kasey looked up and their gazes connected. Studying her face, he decided he wouldn't surgically change a thing about her. She had a perfectly fine face and body and didn't need to lift, tighten, plump or slenderize a single feature.

The surprising thought made him smile. She smiled back and a warm itchy trail began in his chest and headed south.

Kasey knew he was only in Boston for another year, that he planned to move back to California to open his own practice as soon as he finished his fellowship in the American College of Surgeons for Plastic Surgery. He also understood she was facing a potentially debilitating diagnosis regarding Huntington's and probably didn't want to start a serious affair with anyone until she knew what her future held. In other words, she wasn't looking for anything permanent any more than he was.

No strings was the phrase of the day, and the more he thought about it, the better it sounded.

Angie approached with her laptop opened, interrupting his thoughts. "Mr. O'Leary's here," she said, her eyes tight as if the fluorescent lights were too bright.

"Thanks," he said, taking the computer. "Send him right in."

Kasey didn't like the way Franklin looked, noticeably thinner and with the abdomen back to protruding as it had before. He was also pale and grimacing as if in pain. She jumped up to help him into the exam room. His skin felt clammy yet cold.

"Are you okay?" she asked.

"Just a bit short of breath today is all," he said, maintaining a charming façade. The thought of what they'd have to tell him later made her heartsick.

"Have a seat on the gurney and I'll take your temperature." She rolled over the stand containing the all-in-one blood-pressure cuff, thermometer, and pulse oximeter, and applied them all. A short time later she saw his temperature and pulse were elevated, and his blood pressure and oxygen were down. She grabbed a nasal cannula and hooked him up to the wall oxygen while they waited for Jared.

Franklin pressed his palm against his sternum and rubbed.

"What's happening?" Kasey asked.

He shook his head, grimacing again. "Feels like I've got heartburn. Felt like it all day."

She should have thought of it the moment he'd

walked in with pale diaphoretic skin and complaints of feeling queasy. The man might be having a heart attack. She opened the exam-room door and called out. "Vincent, can you do an EKG for me, stat?"

That request brought both Jared and Vincent barreling into the room. Vincent pushed the EKG machine with him, and while he set up the procedure, Kasey explained to Jared what she thought was going on, and told Angie to call an ambulance.

Two minutes later, Jared read the twelve-lead EKG and found early ST elevation.

"We're going to admit you to the hospital, Franklin. You're most likely having a heart attack, or you've had a silent MI in the past."

No sooner had Jared said it than Franklin grabbed his chest and groaned. "Ooh, make this stop. The pain. Ooh."

Switching to cardiac-arrest mode, Vincent rushed the crash cart into the room and Angie confirmed the paramedics were on their way. Kasey, Vincent and Jared worked like mad as a team to start an IV, deliver needed medicine, and prevent a full-out arrest. Jared ran the near code with confidence and precision, postponing and possibly preventing more heart damage for Franklin O'Leary.

Fifteen minutes later, having received emergency medication through his IV, and with Franklin stabilized, though nowhere near out of danger, the ambulance arrived. Jared gave a report that was rapid though amazingly thorough. He'd obviously been involved in a number of codes over his career. He also got on the phone and called in a report, speaking directly to the attending ER doc. Under instructions from the nearby emergency department, the paramedics transported a semiconscious Franklin to the hospital. Today, the least of his worries had turned out to be the paracentesis fluid with cancer cells.

Just when Kasey thought she could take a deep breath and relax, she saw Mrs. Nunez in her wheelchair in the waiting room with her caretaker at her side. Carla, the caretaker, had called earlier saying Mrs. Nunez hadn't urinated all day. The eighty-year-old lady's recent stroke had caused her to retain her urine and she needed occasional straight catheterization. This time Kasey had received a phone order from the woman's geriatric doctor to insert a catheter bag and leave it in place.

Kasey met and greeted her patient and rolled her down the hall to the examination room for the procedure.

Twenty minutes later, having given thorough instructions to the caretaker and after typing up her notes, Kasey returned to her desk. Jared was nowhere to be seen, and a blip of disappointment settled over her as she sat.

Her day was over, the surge of adrenaline from Franklin's cardiac emergency had receded and she was left feeling drained yet restless. She straightened her desk and shut down her computer as she rolled her shoulders to fend off the tension. Warm and sturdy hands that definitely didn't belong to Vincent caressed the lower part of her neck and shoulders. They methodically squeezed, strong thumbs running up her cervical spine.

"Where were you?" she asked, sounding as if she'd died and gone to heaven.

"I was in the back, finishing my consult and admitting orders."

Kasey smiled and let her head drop forward as Jared

proved to be a master at upper-body massage. She'd really like to keep him around for awhile.

"How about I take you home and buy you some dinner?" he said.

The invitation seemed out of the blue, but with his soothing finger ministrations on her aching muscles, right about now he could talk her into skateboarding downhill blindfolded, as long as he didn't stop the magic.

"Sounds like a great idea."

Someone cleared their throat. Kasey looked up. It was Vincent with a "gotcha" glance teetering on a smile. "I restocked the crash cart and Angie cleaned the patient rooms, so we'll be going. Have a good night." He emphasized "night".

"Okay, thanks. See you tomorrow."

"Later, guys," Jared chimed in. "Goodnight, Angie."

Once they'd cleared the door and heard the lock click, Jared leaned over and kissed the back of Kasey's neck, releasing a basketload of tiny tingles up and down her spine. She knew it was a bad idea, because she could get used to this, used to Jared's soft lips delivering pure pleasure into her malnourished sex life. Once she let down her guard, she'd be susceptible to more feelings, and feelings led to pain. But he was still kissing her and she really didn't want him to stop. Not now.

When his hands reached beneath her breasts and cupped them, a tiny ragged sigh escaped her lips and her mind gave up every last annoying thought. He nibbled her earlobe while lifting and running his thumbs over her erect nipples. *Listen to your body, not your mind.* Warmth pooled between her legs, soon turning to an impatient burn. She turned her head to meet his lips. His mouth covered hers and she quickly found his tongue, amazed how easily he'd turned her from a diligent, exhausted NP into a sex-starved male fantasy of a naughty nurse. He could do that to her. He worked magic.

Wanting nothing more than her body flush to his, she stood, their lips never breaking contact. His arms enfolded her, and she instantly found his back, pulling him closer. Soon she'd sufficiently raised his polo shirt so she could run her hands over the petal-soft skin of his ribs and back. He found her hips and bottom, first massaging then pulling her tight to his wedge. Knowing he was ready for her, that he wanted her, pushed her longing over the edge. She rubbed against him, sending sparks up her core, stirring up an even stronger desire to be devoured and sated.

At this rate they'd never make it home, and she'd never in her life expected to make love in the clinic. Had never even fantasized about it. Yet here she was. With Jared. Giving nonverbal consent.

In a rush he pulled away and unzipped his jeans, soon tugging at her nursing scrubs, which dropped to the floor in record time. He balanced her hips on the edge of her desk and found her opening with the fingers of one hand, while the other busily dug in his pocket for the foil wrapper. In a flash the protection business got taken care of and, moving her thong out of the way, he entered in a long, smooth thrust. First she expanded to his size as he filled her, then, when she clamped down, an intense shudder rolled through her, long and fathomless. She wrapped her legs around his hips for deeper access and pushed against him, starving for his touch. Each thrust sent a building wave of excitement throughout her body, her heart pounded in her chest, until everything spiraled down to one point of pure pleasure that pulsed and grew until it exploded. With a gasp, her head fell forward onto his shoulder, and she held him tight until he came on a ragged breath and a curse.

"You make me act like a crazy man," he rasped over her ear.

"And I'm as prim as ever," she said, removing her legs from around his waist.

The steamy smile he gave her was genuine and so utterly sexy she had to look away if there was any hope of leaving the office before morning.

## CHAPTER SEVEN

FORTY-FIVE minutes after sex on the desk, Kasey and Jared arrived at her apartment with a box of pizza and were ravenously eating. She noticed Jared tickle Daisy's ears when she passed close enough for him to make contact, and a tenderness she hadn't expected settled inside her. She cautioned herself about letting her guard down, about allowing more feelings to mess up whatever this thing was between them.

His cellphone alarm went off.

"Oh," he said, "give me a minute, would you?" He walked to the kitchen and made a call. "Hi, it's Dad. Just checking in to see if you've done your homework. Good. Any tests this week?"

After Jared finished the call to his twelve-year-old son, Patrick—a call more of few words, grunts, and one-word answers than a real conversation, but which ended in a promise to be at a soccer game on one Sunday morning—Jared said goodbye.

After what seemed like a normal father-son conversation, Jared made another call. "Hi, Chloe, just calling to say goodnight."

Not knowing what else to do and trying not to eavesdrop, Kasey ate more pizza. An odd ache started behind her sternum. Had she ever gotten a call like that, growing up? This man might be a California native, but he had roots right here in Massachusetts with his children. And for the record, she was glad he was here.

From the heartfelt tone in his voice, there was no doubt how much he loved his kids, and she'd bet a thousand dollars his daughter and son adored him, too.

"Goodnight, sugarplum. You keep up the good work, and I'll do my best to get to your soccer game this Saturday afternoon, okay?"

Strolling back to the table, he took a seat and ate another bite of pizza. "Any word from the lab yet?" Jared asked.

"Not yet." She didn't intend to ruin their good time by pursuing that topic. "How'd Chloe do on that test the other day?"

"Got a B-plus."

"Great."

"Did Vincent tell you about his big date?"

"Which one?"

For recently having had mind-blowing sex on a desk, their conversation seemed rather mundane, which made it all the more enjoyable.

"Hey, I see you've got my favorite video game."

She glanced across the room to the box connected to her TV. "Really?" Of course, he had kids so why wouldn't he know about the popular games console? "I use the aerobics program." As if that explained why a thirty-something owned a kid's game.

"That explains why you're in good shape," he said, a knowing smile on his lips.

She had the urge to reach across the table and kiss him, but where would that lead? Besides, she had just taken another bite of pizza. "Thank you." She batted her lashes to accentuate the words around her full mouth.

He winked back, and something stirred inside her.

"I like to bowl. Do you have that one?"

"Of course," she said, putting down her pizza. "I'll challenge you."

"You're on!"

"First I'll need to make your avatar." She wiped some pizza grease from her fingers onto a napkin, and headed across the room.

They spent the next ten minutes playing with the game, creating a small round-headed creature with dark hair and incredible blue eyes that looked amazingly like Jared.

"So that's how you see me, huh?"

"I think I captured your inner essence." She hadn't batted her lashes this much since she was thirteen and had declared her love for Mike Murphy to her six closest friends.

"Yeah, especially the scowling brows."

She laughed. He could take what she dished out, and it made him all the more likeable.

"I've got to tell you, your house is so much homier than mine," he said.

"I've been here a few years, so that's an advantage."

"And you don't rent your furniture." He laughed. "My style of décor is functional." He tossed her a humble look. "I just needed some place to flop yet big enough for the kids to come and stay with me." He glanced around her living room. "My place is a one-bedroom apartment, like yours, but the davenport pulls out into a bed," he said, as he rolled the first virtual ball down the virtual bowling lane. "I bet my kids don't even like coming to stay with me."

"I'm sure they want to be wherever you are."

"Not after this summer."

Rather than continue with the touchy subject, she stood to take her turn and scored a strike.

"Well done," he said.

She curtsied.

"Some time I'll have to take you there."

"Where?

"To my basement apartment. You'd be the only person, besides my kids, I've ever brought there."

Putting it into perspective like that, having the honor of being invited into his private world, she looked at the man she'd had sex with on a desk earlier. On the outside he was gorgeous, seemed confident and was definitely accomplished, yet inside he was just like her, a little insecure and very private. "I'd like that." He'd invited her inside, if only to his apartment. Maybe she'd take him up on it. "Thank you," she said as she rolled her second strike in the bowling game.

Forty minutes later, after several games of bowling, with Jared winning the majority, and a couple of tennis matches where Kasey triumphed, they went back to the table. Kasey watched Jared devour two more pieces of pizza while she picked at her crust.

He'd proved to be stellar as a no-strings lover, and she couldn't let feelings mess things up. When he didn't look so serious and earnest his eyes were sweet and friendly. She thoroughly enjoyed playing the video game with him, having him in her house, sharing a meal, keeping her company. She took a bite of pizza and thought what a striking man he was, and how she'd seen every part of him, and nothing had come close to letting her down. Physically.

Again, that caution flag waved in her mind.

Men didn't stick around in her life. She had to remember that. He wouldn't either. She would be nothing more than a pleasant way station on his journey through Boston. What could she expect from a man with rented furniture? That cold, in-your-face fact changed the taste of the pizza, as it turned from delicious comfort food into cardboard with sauce.

She got up from the table and went into the kitchen to gather her thoughts. Who knew what her future held? She really didn't want to blow this one good thing with Jared by being needy or afraid. She wanted to take what she could, for as long as she could. Gulping down some water at the sink, she straightened her shoulders. She deserved to enjoy herself with a man, this man. Jared. She'd enjoy each moment he gave her and be glad about it. When it ended, that would be it. No strings. No emotions. In the meantime, they'd have shared good, thought-free, solid physical contact.

His strong hands cupped her shoulders. The man had an uncanny knack for sneaking up behind her. She inhaled the woods and orange peel scent that had quickly become her favorite aftershave, plus the added touch of mozzarella and basil.

"You okay?" he asked.

"Fine." She bent her head and brushed her cheek over his knuckles. He wrapped his hands around her waist and rested his chin on her shoulder.

"Good. I'm fine, too."

Glancing into the window pane above the sink, she saw their reflections. To someone passing by they'd appear to be a couple, perhaps in love or married. Little would anyone know they were nothing more than convenient lovers.

With that she turned into his embrace and they kissed again, long, slow, lingering kisses, and soon they found their way into her bed, the pizza forgotten in its cardboard holder and the computer game a distant memory.

Jared watched Kasey stretch like a kitten on the mattress after they'd gotten naked. "We've got to quit meeting like this," she said, falling fall short of coy.

"I'm so glad we have," he said spooning close, nibbling her shoulder, examining her colorful hummingbird tattoo on the back of her shoulder. He wrapped his arms around her and pulled her tight to him. "What do you say we just stay here for ever?"

"Someone would have to bring in the pizza when we got hungry."

He smiled into her hair. "Yeah, and I have a special surgery to scrub in on tomorrow."

"Double stacking implants?"

He tweaked her breast in punishment. "No. I'll have you know, I'm on the surgical team for a certain young boy's cleft lip and palate repair."

She sucked in air and glanced over her shoulder. "Really?"

"Without a doubt."

"That's wonderful."

"I know. I'm wonderful."

She jabbed him with her elbow.

"Ouch. Hey. I'm just being honest."

"So humble."

"You bring out the best in me."

"It's a tough job, but someone has to do it." She snuggled her behind against him, his muscles tensed and the heavy, and hot feeling sprang to life once more.

"Oh, look, you're bringing out the best in me again." With desire pooling in his groin, he positioned himself below her bottom between her upper thighs, close enough to feel her moisture. The damp welcome and heady scent made him shudder with longing. When had a woman turned him on so much?

He moved in tighter then changed her position just enough to give him entrance, and soon the only thoughts in his mind were to please Kasey and satisfy his endless need for her.

Kasey woke in the middle of the night, surprised that Jared was still there. A quick glance at the clock told her it was two in the morning. She got up for a bathroom visit, took one step, but her right leg felt like a tree stump. Falling to the floor, she banged her head on the bedpost. Pain sliced through the side of her head. A brief twinkling of stars appeared behind her eyes. Shaken, she rubbed out the ache.

"Are you okay?" Jared's groggy voice came from over the mattress.

"Leg went to sleep. Tried to walk."

He crawled over the bed and hopped to the floor, pushed his hands under her armpits and helped her stand. Her leg gave early signs of waking up, tingles and pins, burning, and discomfort. He kissed her temple where she'd been rubbing.

"Let me help you," he said. "Bathroom or back to bed?"

She pointed to the bathroom, and he practically carried her as she hopped on her one good leg. "That hasn't happened in years." Yet it had happened last night, too.

"I probably threw my leg over you or something."

Right. But when she'd woken up, their bodies hadn't even been touching. Hummingbird-fast panic shot through her, igniting the nerve endings in her chest. Was this an early sign of Huntington's?

Once she'd made it to the bathroom, she decided to

add this to her surprisingly growing list of things for the dreaded upcoming neurology appointment.

When she returned to her room, the light was on and Jared was dressed and ready to leave. He ran fingers through his hair in an attempt to comb it.

"I need to do some preparation for surgery later today. Guess I'll be going."

He'd clicked into doctor mode, and whatever care and concern he'd shown when he'd helped her up had vanished. The man was the king of compartmentalization.

"Okay, well, let me know how it goes."

He walked toward her, pecked her on the nose. "Without a doubt." Then left.

All the great feelings she'd savored during their time together that night wilted. She tried to buck up under her disappointment, but couldn't quite pull it off.

"Wait!" she said, rushing to the kitchen door.

Surprise changed his sleepy expression as he stopped in mid-reach for the knob.

"I've got to turn off the alarm first."

He nodded in understanding. "Thanks." Clearly, there was no concern about any further conversation on his end. Not even a "Talk soon" or "See you later". Not one further peep from him.

He showed no interest in learning the code to her alarm either.

"Goodnight," she said, trying not to notice so much, fighting off a desire to want more.

"'Night."

The guy had stumbled onto a playmate and could she blame him for allowing for some distraction in his otherwise busy and high-stress schedule? She needed to get used to this no-strings fling. When it was good it was very, very good, but when it felt bad, like now, it stank.

Maybe she wasn't cut out for an affair.

The feeling had slowly and painfully returned to her leg, and only a few needle pricks remained in her foot. She tested her toes by wiggling them and rotating her ankle. As Kasey reset the alarm and walked back to her bedroom, a nagging thought caught hold and wouldn't let her free. What would happen if she turned out to have the Huntington's marker?

On Thursday morning, Kasey received a call at the clinic from the bat-bite mom. The mother's worst fears had come true. There was evidence of bat guano in the child's bedroom. Having done her homework, Kasey told the woman there was only a one percent chance of the bat having rabies in this part of the US, but she still recommended that the mother follow up with her daughter's pediatrician as soon as possible.

Vincent kept eyeing Kasey all morning, a tiny knowing twinkle in his eyes. When he brought her a cup of coffee without being asked, she knew she was in for an interrogation.

"You're banging the doc, aren't you?" His smile was sly and lascivious.

"Is that any of your business?"

"Am I not your closest friend?" He stood before her arms akimbo, with an obvious pout. "I have information rights. You've been withholding breaking news."

She sipped the too-hot coffee, squinted her eyes tightly, then drew in a breath. "Okay. Yes," she whispered, worried Angie might hear. "We've sort of done some things."

"Done some things? Like sex?"

She nodded at his incredulous stare.

"Well blow me away! You little harlot."

"Keep your voice down, would you?"

"I want details. All the details. Oh, my God, Doctor Tall, Dark and Gorgeous is bonking my best friend."

"You say one word to anyone and I'll stitch your mouth shut."

He licked his lips. "Sealed. Promise. But, really, how exciting." He squeezed her shoulder then walked away to pick up a blood-pressure cuff, tossed her an envious glance, then moved on.

The way Kasey felt this morning, all mixed up about what was going on between her and Jared, she wasn't the least bit sure there was anything "exciting" about the predicament she'd found herself in. Now that Vincent knew, he'd keep on her about "Has he called you?" "When are you seeing him again?" and she'd have to be honest and tell him, most likely she'd only been a brief fling. It hadn't meant anything. News she'd rather keep to herself.

It would take diligent practice to start believing the mantra about sex with Jared. *It doesn't mean anything. It doesn't mean anything.*

But, with misplaced feelings beginning to surface, she'd have to try.

Late Thursday afternoon Jared sat down for the first time in hours. He stretched out the aching muscles in his legs and shoulders. The cleft lip and partial palate repair with the pediatric surgical specialist had been fascinating. He wouldn't have missed it for anything, and even felt a little proud that he'd been the person to recommend the child for the pro bono services. Which wouldn't have happened if he hadn't been assigned to the Everett Community Clinic.

He loved being a general surgeon, and plastic surgery seemed like a logical option. He believed in what he did, making people look better, feel better with more self-esteem, no matter how unrealistic some of their goals were. He'd given his new studies his best efforts, because he didn't know how to do anything differently in life, but something had obviously been lacking in the satisfaction department. He hadn't realized how much until now. Today, assisting with the toddler's surgery, it had become painfully apparent. Nothing could compare to the way he felt right now. He'd helped change a child's life.

It felt great, and he wanted to share the revelation with someone special.

Smiling, he fished out his cellphone to give Kasey an update.

"Dr. Finch?" one of the circulating OR nurses said. "Dr. Rheingold wants to see you. He's in the doctors' lounge."

Sliding his cellphone back into his pocket, he walked down the hall.

On Friday morning, Kasey got a call she never expected and was nowhere near prepared for.

A pediatrician for Janie DeHart, the bat-bite child, had decided to take the cautious road and had ordered the treatment for rabies. Kasey understood he was going on the theory of better safe than sorry. Literature suggested that any young child or mentally challenged person suspected of having slept in a room with a bat and having evidence of a bite should be treated. The logic had more to do with the inability to explain exactly what had happened. In Janie's case, she'd thought a bird was flying in her room. Maybe it had been a dream, but the tiny bite marks on her shoulder changed everything.

A large part of her didn't believe it was truly neces-

sary to put that child through the horrendous treatment
for rabies, but would she want to risk being wrong?
In this case, liability and potential lawsuits may have
played a part in the decision by her pediatrician.

The Everett Community Clinic had been chosen
to provide the care, since it was close to the patient's
house. The unlucky child would receive the treatment.
She made an appointment for Janie on Monday, hustled to order the rabies immune globulin and rabies
vaccine, then ran back to her computer to study the
procedure for giving the medicine to prevent the rabies virus from infecting the patient. She dreaded how
hard it would be on the little girl to receive the initial
immune globulin followed by four doses of rabies vaccine over fourteen days.

While she had a quiet moment at her desk, she picked
up the phone and called the hospital to check up on
Franklin O'Leary. Patient confidentiality prevented her
from getting a full report, but she'd been assured he'd
been stabilized and was now in the acute care ward.
Now that they'd resolved his heart attack, they'd have
to move on to finding the source of his cancer. She
thought of Franklin's weary, craggy, but friendly face.
How had he managed to get hit with a double whammy?

In full fret mode, Kasey sat at her desk as the phone
rang again. "Everett Community Clinic, how may I
help you?"

"May I speak to Kasey McGowan?"

"I'm Kasey."

"Hi. This is the Genetics lab. We have your results
and wanted to set up an appointment to discuss them."

The floor seemed to drop out from beneath her feet.
A massive influx of adrenaline through her chest, and
pulsing into her ears, made her head swim. Her breath-

ing fell out of sync, and she had to remind herself to inhale…exhale.

Was she ready to handle the results? No! Her hands trembled, barely able to hold the phone to her ear. A fist-sized wad in her throat made it hard to respond.

"Ms. McGowan?" the lab voice said.

She swallowed against the dry lump. "Yes. I'm here."

"Are you available to come in tomorrow morning?"

"Yes," she wiped her brow, already clammy with fear. "Of course. What time?"

# CHAPTER EIGHT

KASEY grasped at Vincent's arm as he passed her desk in the clinic.

"What's wrong? You look white as a sheet."

"My results are in." Her pulse pounded so loudly in her ears she could hardly hear herself.

"The DNA tests?"

She nodded, unable to draw enough breath to speak.

"Are they negative?"

She shrugged. She'd been told at the original lab appointment that they only gave the results in person.

He hugged her tight, pulled back, grabbed her hands, squeezed, and looked deep into her eyes. "When do you find out?"

"Tomorrow," she whispered.

"Do you need me to stay with you tonight? Then we can go to the appointment together in the morning."

She chewed on her lower lip and shook her head. "Just go with me tomorrow, please."

"Of course. I'll be there. All you have to do is tell me when. Now, let me get you some water."

Her heart swelled with love for Vincent for being there for her. Since she only had two friends, she was grateful he was one of them.

The rest of the day went by in a blur. Kasey hardly

remembered how she got home, but somehow she stood in her kitchen with an attention-starved cat circling her ankles.

After she fed Daisy, and scratched her ears until the cat had slipped into oblivion, she ran a hot bath and slid into the soothing water, hoping it might help unjangle her nerves. Tomorrow held her fate. If she had the Huntington gene, she would eventually get the disease, but wouldn't know when the symptoms would begin. She thought about the recent episodes of her leg going numb at night. Had the symptoms already started? If she didn't have the marker, she could take a deep breath and thank the heavens for saving her heartache, physical pain, and a long and sad demise.

She thought about calling Jared—a fleeting thought, as quick as a drip from the faucet into the bathtub. He had enough going on in his life. Besides, their relationship wasn't like that.

In fact, they didn't *have* a relationship. Beyond sex.

His goofy round-headed avatar popped into her mind, and how earnestly he'd bowled the other night, as if holding an actual bowling ball instead of a video game wand.

What they had was sex. Not friendship. Not a relationship. Sex. Pure and simple. A clench of sadness lodged in her chest. It seemed that life-threatening disease and no-strings sex wasn't such a good mix after all.

Besides, Vincent would be here in a flash if she needed him. He was her true friend. And though right now she felt more afraid and lonely than when she'd been a pre-schooler and her mother had left her alone at night to sneak off and see some man, she refused to burden Vincent until tomorrow.

After the long, warm bath, she got into her pajamas

and poured herself a glass of wine. She'd beaten Jared in video tennis the other night, now she'd leave the ball in his court and wait to see how long it would be before he called her. Yes, it was a test, because her phony no-strings self-esteem could use a little perking up.

Walking to the living room, she slipped a DVD into the player for distraction, and took a long sip of her pinot noir.

Now, if she could only make it through the night, tomorrow she'd find out her future. It all boiled down to a Huntington's disease marker at chromosome four, and that tiny thing made her mad as hell.

On Saturday morning, Jared made early post-surgical rounds for his latest implants, facelifts, lipos, and tummy tucks at the surgi-center recovery, finishing in plenty of time to make it to Chloe's soccer game. Back in his office, on a whim, he dialed Kasey to see if she'd like to come along.

The phone rang and rang, and he admitted being glad, since he wasn't sure if it was a good idea to bring someone to his kids' games. In the two years since the divorce, his children had never seen him with another woman. There had been a few, very few…two, to be exact…and neither woman had stood a chance of having a real relationship with him under the circumstances. His ex, on the other hand, had already moved in with her neurosurgeon boyfriend, and Jared sensed it mixed up the kids, who were still dealing with the split-up of their parents. Why should he add to it?

Okay, bad idea. He didn't need to confuse Chloe by bringing Kasey along, especially if they were only having a fling, and the chances were Chloe might never see her again.

When would it ever be a good time to bring someone else into his kids' lives? He wasn't sure, but Kasey had crept into his mind more and more lately, and he suspected she and his kids would get along just fine. And speaking of getting along just fine, last night he would have given anything to wrap his arms around her and snuggle down for sleep…after a long, thorough love-making session.

The admission startled him. Was he thinking of trading in unattached sex for an actual relationship? He rubbed his temple, cellphone against the other ear. Man, he must be going soft at thirty-nine. Maybe he wasn't ready yet. Kasey was just a woman he enjoyed being around, one who could shake him out of his overly serious moods, one who turned him on like wildfire in weeds. All good, but what would that add up to over the long haul?

The phone continued to ring. Not having to call was supposed to be the beauty of a no-strings affair. So why did he want to talk to Kasey this morning? Simply to hear her voice?

He stared out the second-story window onto the parking lot, not in the least bit sure what to do about Kasey.

Once he heard the voicemail beep on her cellphone he quickly thought about hanging up, but cleared his throat instead. "Hi, it's Jared. I'm heading out for the kids' soccer games and I wanted to touch base. I, uh, just want to wish you a good weekend. I know it's a little tough for you these days, but hang in there, okay?" He hung up, shaking his head. How lame was that? He ought to be embarrassed for such a pitiful pep talk. Some smooth operator he'd turned out to be.

He walked to the elevator and to his car for the two-hour drive by himself, knowing his thoughts would be with Kasey part of the way. Maybe he'd try to call her later, see what she'd been up to all weekend. Could he do that with this no-strings thing? He shook his head and decided to concentrate on his kids instead.

He'd spend the night near the kids' school and stick around for Patrick's game on Sunday morning then head home. He needed a good night's sleep so he could start the mentorship with the head of Pediatric Plastic Surgery for the next two weeks. After the cleft lip and palate surgery the other day, it was a specialty he found surprisingly intriguing, and one more thing he felt compelled to share with Kasey.

Maybe he would call her later.

Kasey rushed into the genetics lab with Vincent by her side. "I'm Kasey McGowan. You have some results for me?"

The receptionist wrote down her name and walked to a cabinet, fingers walking through the files. Soon he found and retrieved a white envelope, returned to the counter, and made a call. While the phone rang he asked, "Do you have a neurology appointment scheduled?"

"Yes," she said, hands noticeably trembling, her mouth drying by the second.

"Hi," the technician said into the phone. "I have Ms. McGowan here for her test results." He hung up the phone. "Ms. Jamal, our genetic counselor, will be with you shortly."

How hard could it be? She either had the genetic marker or she didn't. She didn't need to wait for a special counselor to tell her that.

Kasey wanted to reach for and tear open the envelope with flapping, unruly hands and fingers. She wanted to slide out the report, then open the tri-folded sheets and read the results right that instant. Why did she have to wait?

With her entire body sensing the wildly ragged rhythm from her heart, and her mouth as dry as sand, she did her best to stay calm and patient on the outside.

A tall doctor, with huge brown eyes and a long face and nose, appeared and quietly offered her hand. "I'm Naali Jamal, won't you follow me?" She took the envelope from the technician and led the way to a sequestered corner office.

"I hear you are a medical professional, Ms. McGowan?"

"Yes," Vincent answered for her. "She's a nurse practitioner."

The office was smartly decorated and tastefully furnished, but Kasey couldn't take in details. With Vincent by her side, she sat. He took her hand and squeezed.

The young woman carefully opened the envelope and withdrew the contents. She unfolded the paper and studied the results. Her brows minutely drew together, giving Kasey another rush of adrenaline.

"Hmm," the woman said, before looking up from the report. "Let me show you the results, and explain what they mean."

Both Kasey and Vincent sat forward on their seats to see the report more closely, but she didn't immediately share the test sheet.

"What we look for with this test is the number of CAG repeats. That's cytosine-adenine-guanine. If the repeats are under twenty-eight, you do not have the marker. Between twenty-nine and thirty-four CAG repeats, you won't develop Huntington's disease, but the next generation is still at risk. Between thirty-five and thirty-nine, some individuals will develop HD, and the next generation is also at risk. Equal to or greater than forty, and the individual will definitely get HD. There's just no telling when, and more tests are needed to tell if the symptoms have already begun. That's why we send you to a neurologist."

Lord, could she drag this out any longer? Kasey's foot tapped the air faster than hummingbird wings.

"And what is Kasey's result?"

Ms. Jamal cleared her throat. "Thirty-nine."

Kasey's body went slack in the chair. She'd been tense so long that the borderline result had caught her off guard. "Thirty-nine!" she blurted. "What percentage of people will get Huntington's disease with a result of thirty-nine?"

"Again, it is hard to make this call. More testing will help identify if there is early evidence of the disease. Continued follow-up would be necessary."

"For the rest of my life?"

"Perhaps."

One CAG repeat away from certain disease left her dangling over life's genetic craps shoot. She didn't know whether to be relieved or looking over her shoulder every day for the dark, haunting shadow of Huntington's disease sneaking up on her.

Good heavens. Not knowing if she'd be one of the people in the thirty-five to thirty-nine results range to develop the disease turned out to be worse than knowing for sure that with time she'd succumb to the disorder. The never knowing for sure would drive her crazy, if she let it.

Kasey's hand flew to her mouth. She tried not to whimper, but couldn't stop the sound leaving her throat. "How is a person supposed to live like this?"

"We can make an appointment with a therapist for you."

"A therapist?" She shook her head. "I'm supposed to sit around and talk about my feelings about how horrendous life is and why did I get stuck with this non-diagnosis? No, thanks. That's not for me." Angry about her results, she'd lashed out and immediately regretted it, but she wasn't about to spend the rest of her life worrying. What was the point?

"It's for support, Kasey," Vincent said. "At least think about it."

She sighed, sorry she'd chastised the genetic counselor and her best friend. "I know, you're right, it couldn't hurt to have all the support I can get. If you give me the card, Ms. Jamal, I'll check my schedule and make an appointment as soon as possible."

The woman nodded her approval as she proffered the business card.

"Can we move her neurology appointment up?" Vincent spoke up.

"I'll see what I can do," Ms. Jamal said, glancing over the computer screen. "I'll send the neurologist an e-mail, but I can't guarantee anything."

With her hands cupping her cheeks, Kasey stared at her now perfectly still feet. How could she be so unlucky? They couldn't even tell her for sure if she'd get the disease symptoms. And she sure as hell would never have kids to pass down the curse. She'd never thought that much about having children of her own, but knowing she didn't have an option hurt, like a knife to her chest. She shook her head, knocking over warm tears onto her cheeks from her brimming lids. She'd thought life had sucked yesterday. Today she'd entered a whole new realm of suckiness.

\* \* \*

"I'd like another beer," Kasey said to the server at the harbor-side café. "You know what?" she said to Vincent. "Let's take one of those amphibious tours. I've lived near Boston my whole life and have never taken a tour of the city. What do you say?"

"Sure. I left today completely open for you."

She squeezed his forearm, already feeling the warm fuzzy feeling from the first drink. "I love you, guy."

"Don't go all sappy on me or I'll cut you off the beer."

Kasey dug into her seafood salad, quietly vowing to grab the gusto in life since she didn't have a choice about her health status. A stinking diagnosis with an iffy future was not going to keep her from enjoying the here and now. All things considered, she felt fine today, physically. No aches. No pains. She'd gotten out of bed that morning with everything working fine. She squinted into the sun at Vincent's silhouette, so glad he was there with her.

Riffling through her purse for a tissue, she glanced at her phone—she'd had it turned off all morning, knowing she'd be at the lab. There was a voice message, and she listened as Jared wished her a good weekend. His awkward and businesslike message made her heart clutch the tiniest bit; just knowing he'd thought about her today, well, somehow it mattered. Not good, she reminded herself. She wasn't supposed to care.

"Who was that?" Vincent asked.

"Jared."

Vincent's brows shot up. "Your hot, hunky hero?"

"Knock it off, will you?"

He grinned at her and she took another bite of salad.

"Maybe later we can do the Boston history walk, too," she said, since she had a captive for the day. "I haven't done that since grade school."

Vincent shrugged. "Whatever you want."

"Thanks."

What she really wanted to do was call Jared back and invite him over for some mind-numbing sex, some help-me-forget-about-all-the-bad-luck-in-life lovemaking, but first she needed to figure things out. Should she tell him her results and risk gaining his pity, or keep her diagnosis to herself and take a chance that he'd resent her for it? He'd said himself not to expect results for up to six weeks, so she had time to think things through. He didn't need to know how she'd spent her Saturday morning.

Her second ice-cold beer arrived and she took a sip. "What was the name of that guy you said gives great haircuts?"

"Arturo?"

"Yeah, can you get me an appointment with him? I need some new style or something."

"Of course I can get you in. We're like this." Vincent crossed his fingers.

"Fantastic." She stabbed a plump piece of shrimp from her salad, thinking it was the best-tasting lunch she'd ever had.

One thing was clear—she wasn't going to hole up in her house and waste one second on feeling sorry for herself. From now on,it would be all about living each day as if it were her last. That's what a CAG score of thirty-nine had taught her.

Jared slowed down his car on Sunday night and rolled toward Kasey's house. He'd had the opportunity to go with Patrick's team for a victory lunch after the soccer game and hadn't passed it up. After lunch had come ice-cream treats and a chance to take Chloe along. When the school didn't seem opposed to him being there, he took advantage of more time with his kids. He knew his ex wouldn't mind as he was allowed every other weekend plus one weeknight for visitation per their standard California divorce settlement. Truth was, since Patrice was only able to fly out once a month to visit their kids, she was fine with Jared visiting as often as possible. The problem was, he couldn't make time often enough with his work schedule and his plastic surgery training.

Soon it had been the dinner hour, and again he'd gotten the okay from the school to take the kids out for another meal. It had been a long but enjoyable two days, and he looked forward to doing it all over again next weekend. The thought of his kids not being around after the summer gave him a dull ache in his chest.

The lights at Kasey's house were on, but the blinds were closed. He glanced at his watch. It wasn't that late, nine o'clock. His better judgment told him he should have called before he'd left and that showing up unannounced wouldn't be acceptable no matter how easygoing Kasey was. But, boy, did he want to. She'd awakened a beast inside him, and nothing but her sexy kisses and soft body could tame it.

He sat in his running car, staring at her house. He could make out her silhouette on the blinds. It looked like she was standing and holding something—a guitar? Maybe she was playing that video game again, and she'd like some company. Headlights came up the street behind him. Kicking his inner censor, he pressed on the gas and drove past quickly, hoping she wouldn't happen to notice his schoolboy antics. Some "no-strings" lover he'd turned out to be. Man, he needed to get it together where Kasey was concerned.

\* \* \*

On Monday morning, Kasey went to work dreading facing poor Janie DeHart. Her experience with childhood immunizations reminded her it wouldn't be easy. Kids could freak out and flail about like slippery fish when scared. These shots would be like giving a flu vaccination, they needed to go into deep muscle and the after-effect would feel like someone had punched her in the arm. Once Janie realized how painful the first shot was, her mother would have to drag her into the clinic, kicking and screaming, for the four follow-up appointments. Still, this revised and updated treatment was far, far better than the old twenty-three to thirty injections in the abdomen. The worst side-effect to watch for was the same with any immunization—anaphylaxis. Other than that, the side effects should be mild—headache, nausea, sometimes vomiting. If Janie worked herself into a fit, she might vomit anyway.

Kasey remembered hearing about rabies treatment as a kid, as though it was an urban legend, greatly embellished to scare kids out of their sneakers. In her childhood mind's eye she'd seen evil nurses coming at her with foot-long needles and scowls on their faces. The fear factor had ranked right up there with stepping on a rusty nail and getting "lock jaw." Oh, what her child's mind could do with a little information and a lot of imagination back in her day.

Kasey would do her best not to be that scary nurse for Janie, and to put both the child and mother at ease. She hoped she could make the unfortunate appointment as tolerable as possible.

Angie appeared at her desk. "The DeHarts are here."

Kasey fought back a tiny wave of nervous energy. She'd been a nurse for almost ten years—she'd take control of the situation and make sure nothing got out of hand. In theory, everything should work out fine. In theory.

Kasey stood and called for Vincent. "I'm going to need your help with this. Can you bring in the patient while I prepare the vaccines?"

"Of course."

"Oh, and can you have some epinephrine on hand in case she has an adverse reaction?"

"Gotcha."

"I may need you to hold her down, too."

"I know, I know. Kids love me. I'll make faces at her, get her laughing, then you can slip in with your shots. She won't even know what hit her."

A half-hour later, surprisingly, Vincent's predictions had panned out. Janie got a little antsy while Kasey removed the old dressing to examine the small puncture wounds on her shoulder, but she quickly fell under Vincent's spell.

Now Kasey patted the whimpering child on the head and let her pick the biggest and brightest sticker, plus two lollipops. The relieved Mrs. DeHart looked on with grateful, watery eyes. Kasey nodded at her after a subtle exhalation. "We'll get through this."

"Thank you," Mrs. DeHart mouthed to Kasey, then to Janie she said, "Are you ready for those chocolate-chip pancakes I promised?"

"Yes!" The little girl tugged the air with the fist of her non-shot arm, preferring to hold the other one perfectly still and stiff as if bionic. After waiting twenty minutes, while Vincent did his *Sesame Street* imitations, there had been no signs of adverse reaction.

The bat-bite area was slowly healing, though still red. She'd had Vincent clean the area and put on a new bandage for good measure. Now the little girl was good to go.

Kasey didn't want to push the point, but since the regimen of shots was days one, three, seven, fourteen and twenty-eight, they'd be repeating the process again in three days. Hopefully, all would go just as well as it had today.

# CHAPTER NINE

KASEY didn't waste any time grabbing life by the tail. She got off work early Monday evening and took the T to the Chinatown station, took a brisk walk to Boston Public Garden and cut over to Newbury Street to get her hair cut and styled by Vincent's friend Arturo. She never grew tired of the beautiful nineteenth-century brownstones along these tree-lined streets. Her favorite trees were the magnolias down towards the other end of the eclectic European-style shopping area.

She'd eaten before she'd left work, but the rows and rows of outdoor cafés filled to overflowing with customers on this warmer spring evening were inviting, nevertheless. Something on the table she'd just passed was rich with garlic and herbs and made her mouth water.

Skipping down the steps to the lower-level salon, she crossed her fingers Arturo would do well by her. At his this price, he'd better. While she waited for her appointment in the high-tech salon, mildly distracted by strange scents of chemical and hair products, so different from outdoors, she read the local newspaper, wondering if the fumes could be hazardous to her health.

One story caught her eye: "Conjoined Twins Await Delicate Surgery". As she read the story about the twins joined at the head, the article mentioned the children were at the general hospital, where a world-renowned on-staff neurosurgeon had performed a similar surgery several years before.

"Kasey?" A Hollywood pop-goth styled young woman approached. Her edgy multilayered hairdo, including stair-step bangs, and make-up resembling a raccoon, fascinated Kasey. "Arturo is ready for you."

As Kasey followed the click-clicking of the assistant's black stiletto boots toward Arturo's station, Kasey promised she wouldn't get talked into any strange new haircut. Classic was what she had in mind, and if she explained herself well enough, classic was what Arturo should deliver.

Two and a half hours later, Kasey left the hair salon with new lift in her step, probably due to the significantly lighter pocketbook. With hair cut to her shoulders, brilliantly shaped and styled but with just enough edge to stand out, she held her head high, even touching up her usual lip gloss to add to the look. She checked her cellphone to see if anyone had called and kicked herself for hoping Jared might have. No such luck.

As she walked further down the trendy street, she passed a particularly well-manicured spring garden in front and a brightly lit bay window on the first floor. There, on display, was a leopard-patterned sleeveless dress with a Mandarin collar, straight skirt, and a wide black belt. It snagged her attention and held it. Wow, would she dare wear something like that, so different than her usual practical style? She stood beside the pink and white impatiens and spent all of three seconds making her decision.

Her new "why not" attitude was taking hold. If she wasn't careful, she could get used to living like there was no tomorrow. After pushing through the door of the boutique-sized store, she asked for her size in the dress, and then smiled on her way into the fitting room. If Jared had the good sense to call her in the next day or two, she'd model the outfit for him then, if he was lucky, she'd help him remove it.

Wednesday's bat vaccination appointment went similarly to the first, with the exception of Janie being more apprehensive and needing to be bribed into going inside the examination room. Vincent played tic-tac-toe with her while Kasey prepared the shot. Just as she finished with the injection, Angie told her she had a call. Without giving the call a thought, she returned to her desk and answered.

"Hey, good lookin', how've you been?"

"Jared." A pleasant burst of tiny flappy things behind her breastbone made her smile. She couldn't let him know what he did to her. "Long time no hear from," she said in a more modulated tone. She cradled the phone between her ear and shoulder as she shuffled through a pile of messages on her desk, trying to sound businesslike and not to let the migrating nest of jitters in her tummy take over.

"You miss me?"

It sounded like he was smiling. Give him the upper hand? No way would she admit exactly how much she'd missed him since last week. "Maybe."

"Good. Can I take you to dinner tonight?"

She thought of her new dress and how much he'd like it, how he'd give her that lean and hungry look after feasting his eyes on her. Plus the fact that she really wanted to see him. "That would be nice."

"Great. I'll pick you up at seven."

"Sounds good. See you then." For once he'd called

first. Actually asked her out on a date. She hung up,
dinner deal all ironed out, beaming.

Of course Vincent caught her with the goofy smile.
"Uh-huh," he said, nodding his head as if he were a
sleuth solving a case.

At five p.m. Jared finished the rhinoplasty consultation on the fifteen-year-old boy and headed back to his
shared office to type up his notes. Wesley Rheingold
met him in the corridor.

"I've got some breaking news," he said. "The conjoined twins have been deemed stable enough to un-
dergo surgery and Elwood Fairchild is ready to go."

Dr. Fairchild was the world renowned neurosurgeon
who had performed one of the very first conjoined-at-
the-head twin surgeries in the United States several
years back.

"Fantastic. Any chance I can observe some of the
surgery?" Thinking it would be tomorrow before anything got under way.

"Observe? No, my good man. One of the scheduled
assisting surgeons is sick and contagious with flu. So
I've gone one step further and made you part of team
two, plastic surgery. Once Fairchild has completed the
head, brain, and great vessels separation, each twin
will have their own team to reconstruct their scalps and
foreheads. We need all the manpower we can get, and
I've watched you work. You'll be a great addition. We'll
work in shifts, as this surgery will take anywhere from
eighteen to thirty-six hours. Are you willing to help?"

"How can I refuse?" Just thinking about the major
opportunity gave Jared goose-bumps. He'd never
dreamed of being a part of something like this, something great and life-altering. "Of course I want to!"

"Great. Then grab your stuff, it's time to scrub in."

Jared jumped at the chance to make history. With all thoughts focused on the twins and the surgery, he followed Dr. Rheingold down the hall toward the OR. Totally stoked, as he'd said back home in California when he'd been a teenager. Then it hit him: he needed to let Kasey know he couldn't make their date tonight. He rushed to keep in pace with his colleague as he fished out his cellphone. Deep in the heart of the solidly built hospital there wasn't a signal. He grimaced, knowing he'd have a lot of explaining to do to Kasey later, but opportunity and history called, and he followed Dr. Rheingold into the OR.

Kasey checked her watch for the third time. It was now nine o'clock. Jared's cell went directly to voicemail. She shook her head. All dressed up and with no one to see her, she felt foolish. And angry.

To hell with it.

To hell with him!

She picked up her rock musician video guitar and switched on the TV monitor with plans to get lost with her second-favorite pastime after making love with Jared, playing lead fake guitar in seventies rock classics.

It felt far too familiar to be left dangling by a man without the common courtesy of a call. With her last break-up, her boyfriend had taken off with another woman and had gotten in touch with Kasey as an afterthought three weeks later. She'd never allow that feeling again. Not if she could help it. Smack in the middle of a Pink Floyd classic, things got blurry and she started missing notes, which knocked her expert status back toward novice. She gave up, sliding the strap for the mock guitar from her shoulder and turning off the game.

She marched down the hall, took off her new dress and put on a baggy T-shirt and flannel PJ bottoms. She didn't have time for this any more. Her last boyfriend had called her clingy and insecure. Well, she'd never give a man the chance to say that about her again. As far as she was concerned, Jared Finch had just severed the non-existent strings of their superficial relationship.

Thirty-six hours after the opening incision, two sedated and separated toddlers lay in their own cribs, each whole. The team of two dozen neuro and plastic surgeons, and nearly as many OR nurses, all equal parts exhausted and elated, congratulated themselves on a job well done.

With the monitoring equipment, heart and breathing machines pushed aside in an obstacle-course manner, discarded sheets and blankets cast off in piles, overflowing hampers, and bloodied basins and surgical instruments filling the stainless-steel sinks, the OR looked like a war zone.

Jared rubbed his neck and checked his watch. It was five a.m. Friday morning. There was only one person he wanted to talk to. The surgery had been a game changer, to use Kasey's term. It had revived his love of the intricate, helpful, healing art of surgery. Yes, he'd understood what cosmetic procedures could do for patients, but it didn't put the fire in his belly like this type of surgery did. The experience had convinced him to change his plastic surgery focus from strictly cosmetic to a more intense specialty, pediatric repair. Kasey had figured out he wasn't really happy with his chosen course before he'd even admitted it to himself. He couldn't wait to share the news with her.

Kasey!

He'd stood her up, would have to face her certain disdain, yet he still wanted to see her. He strode toward the doctors' lounge for a quick shower, after which he planned to head over to her house to see her before she left for work. If he was lucky, he'd be early enough and she'd still be in bed.

Kasey came out of a deep sleep and heard what sounded like ice cubes clinking in a glass. She shook her head, listened, and heard it again. Was it raining? Or hailing? That didn't make sense. The sound came in spurts. What the heck was going on?

"Kasey!" She heard a muffled version of her name from outside the window. "Kasey!" This time it was more like a strained whisper.

More ice tinkling.

She sat bolt upright, pushing her hair out of her eyes, and leaned toward the window near the bed. Lifting the blind, she peeked beneath. Jared! In the bushes under her bedroom window, he stood looking disheveled and super-tired. Had he been on a binge for two days? More importantly, what was he doing here now?

He saw her and waved, pointed to his chest, then to the other side of her house. The door. "Let me in," he mouthed.

Was he crazy? Stand her up on Wednesday night without the courtesy of a call, no word the next day, then show up at her house at stupid o'clock on Friday and expect to be let in?

Oh, gosh, he was bending to grab more pebbles. She tapped on the window and waved her hands back and forth in the international sign for "Enough. Please stop that".

He pointed toward the back door again, looking earnest. Oh, hell. She dropped the blind and scrubbed her face, walking—more like stumbling as if half-asleep, which she was—to the kitchen entrance. It was six o'clock, and there he was, standing on the steps, sports jacket open and shirt tails hanging beneath, his hair finger-combed at best. There were deep, dark circles beneath his eyes, like the sign of a madman, yet the blue velvet shone through the thick outline of his lashes as if a beacon. She had to be crazy to let him in. Yet she wanted to.

Once she'd punched in the release code on the alarm system she opened the door.

He burst through, eyes bright, cheeks flushed, face animated. "You won't believe what I've been doing the last two days."

In no mood to play guessing games, she gave him Ms. Daisy's favorite cat-eye glare. "Were you in jail for public drunkenness?" Her deadpan reply fell flat. "Because that's what you look like."

He bent his head, chin to chest, looking at himself. "Sorry." Suddenly distracted by her, he gave a probing gaze from head to fuzzy slippers, then back to her face. "Your hair's longer on one side than the other."

She screwed up her face. "It's supposed to be that way. Now, are you going to tell me where you've been the last two days or are we going to discuss my latest hair fashion?"

He leaned one elbow on her countertop. "I was part of the conjoined twins surgery! You know, the little girls who've been plastered all over the news the last six weeks? Them!"

She'd heard of them, joined at the forehead, sharing part of each other's brain.

"I was on one of the plastic surgery teams," he said, standing tall.

"Wait a second. I'm not awake yet. You were what?"

"I got to be part of the team of surgeons. It was fantastic." He practically danced around the room while telling her about his good fortune. "I haven't slept in two days, but I'm high as a kite about this. I finally figured out what I want to do with my plastic surgery fellowship. Sure, I was committed to be the best cosmetic surgeon I could be, making people look their best, giving them a new lease on life...but something kept nagging at me, that maybe this wasn't what I really wanted or needed to do. You noticed that, too, didn't you? It didn't grab me by the soul and say, hey, this is what you were made for, but this type of surgery sure as hell did. It was like a huge breakthrough, and—" He stopped long enough to take her all in again. "It was my game changer, and you're the first person I wanted to tell."

He let her stare at him, a long, sober stare as she digested the significance of that remark. In return, he grinned at her, waiting.

"I'm the first person you wanted to tell?"

He nodded, stepping closer. She backed up, leaving no room between her and the kitchen sink. He'd finished a cut-and-dried monologue on professional fulfillment, changing from cosmetic leaning to a reconstructive slant, and he'd still somehow managed to break into her heart and do a different kind of repair. The kind of game change that helped a girl, this girl, open up to new and exciting possibilities. She couldn't dare let him know what was running through her mind.

"But you stood me up Wednesday night. You didn't even call."

He shook his head, his eyes begging for understanding. "No, no, no. I was at work, getting ready to leave for our date, when they grabbed me. Well, Dr. Rheingold grabbed me at the last minute. I tried to call but couldn't get a signal. Time was of the essence. It wasn't like I could run outside and make the call first."

"Really?"

"Honestly. If I could've, I would've."

This was either the biggest and best excuse she'd ever heard for being stood up, or Jared really meant it. She didn't live with her head under a rock. She'd read the newspaper headlines yesterday about the dramatic surgery in progress. He looked totally sincere, and since his life-changing soliloquy had touched her so deeply, she decided to give him the benefit of the doubt. "Are you freaking pulling my leg, or are you serious about all of this life-changing stuff?"

"Serious as a heart attack." It really was obvious. Of course he was telling the truth. Of course he'd made a major decision about the direction of his career. He'd even used her term, a game changer. Of course he'd wanted to tell her first. All she had to do was look into his captivating blue eyes to know that.

He opened his arms to welcome her in. It seemed like the right thing to do—come on, the guy was practically a hero—so she stepped into his embrace, immediately amazed by how right he felt. And how great—solid chest, heat radiating from beneath his shirt, all lean muscle and strength.

"So what are you waiting for? Tell me all about the surgery."

"Put on some coffee and I will." She could tell he didn't want to let go, but he did.

Jared watched Kasey move purposefully around the kitchen, opening a cupboard here and a drawer there as she gathered the coffee, a filter, and two mugs. She wore a slinky wraparound daisy yellow robe that tied at the waist and accentuated her curves, and he thought he might like to see her in it on a regular basis. The thought made his mouth go dry. "May I have a drink of water?"

"Of course, help yourself to anything," she said, filling the coffee maker with water.

He moved behind her and put his free hand on her hip as he filled his glass with the other and drank from the tap water. Damn she felt fantastic. "You realize that's a loaded invitation."

*Help himself to anything.*

She glanced over her shoulder and smiled. He put down his glass, lifted her hair and kissed the side of her neck. "For the record, I like the new uneven look. Makes me want to put my fingers in your hair and mess it all up."

She held perfectly still as he placed light kisses up and down her long neck, as her silken skin beneath his lips rose in tiny bumps. He wrapped his arms around her center and pulled her close to his arousal, then nuzzled her ear with his nose, wanting nothing more than to plant himself inside her. Drained from two days without sleep, yet still mightily turned on by Kasey, he asked the question front and center in his mind.

"Will you go back to bed with me?" he said, his voice raspy with desire.

Her head came up, her shoulders back. He felt her inhale and her spine go board stiff. Disappointed by the change in body language, he waited for a rejection. But he was being honest, as honest as it got. He wanted her, with all his heart. Her denying him would hurt to the core.

How bold could he be and still expect results? Could

he blame her for kicking him out of her kitchen? He'd stood her up, shown up at the crack of dawn, and now wanted to take her to bed. He held his breath, preparing for the worst.

"Yes," she whispered.

Jared made long, slow love to Kasey, and if she wasn't careful she'd interpret it as committed lover sex. Through his fingers and lips he'd told a tale of deep attraction, admiration, and wonder. His thighs and pelvis followed up with bold, uninhibited desire on a mission for satisfaction. As always, her body responded to each touch, slowly building tension, sometimes unbearably so, and longing for release, fighting for it with every fiber in her body. Though he seemed to have read her mind on so many levels, he hadn't been afraid to ask what she'd wanted, meeting whatever need she'd had— Do you want me to touch you there? Like this? Is that good?—until he'd brought her to the limit and she'd shuddered beneath him.

No man could make love like this without caring. Could he? With his head above hers, his eyes probing deeply into hers, his heated, hooded look went beyond sex—it spoke of connection and broken-down barriers. Intimacy. Of that she was certain.

It sent shivers through her, and she saw the satisfaction on his face when he noticed as she delved into those inviting blue eyes and soon got lost in the sensations.

Her release was so strong it opened a gate she'd been guarding with all her heart. With each spasm of climax tears welled in her eyes. Stripped down to the rawest of feelings, through Jared's meticulous lovemaking, Kasey couldn't control her crying.

"What's wrong? Did I hurt you?" He rolled off her and came back up on his elbow.

She shook her head, pulling the sheet to her face to wipe away the tears.

"Sweetheart, what's up?"

She pulled away from him, embarrassed by being so obvious. He spooned behind her, his hand and fingers splayed across her stomach. He hooked his chin over her shoulder.

"Tell me," he whispered.

After hesitating, not wanting his pity, she changed her mind about keeping the information to herself. The weight had become unbearable. "I got the results."

His hand tightened over her waist. "And?"

"I'm as close as you can get to being positive for Huntington's without getting complete confirmation."

"Come again?" He pulled her onto her back so he could look at her face. A shadow of sadness and confusion covered his eyes.

She explained everything the genetic counselor had told her. How she might or might not develop the symptoms of Huntington's over her lifetime, and how her offspring could also develop the disease.

"I never really thought about having children, but now that I've been told I shouldn't." More tears brimmed. She shook her head. "I hate not having options. I hate wondering if I'm going to get sick and lose everything I've worked for my whole life."

He kissed her forehead. "Sweetheart, you're only thirty-two. You'll have your whole life ahead of you."

"How do you know that? Are you God? I could develop this vile disease next week, tomorrow even."

He enveloped her in his embrace, rocked her gently, and kissed her hair.

Pain sliced through her core. She'd been given a damning diagnosis, or non-diagnosis, depending on how she interpreted it, and she'd fallen in love with a man, a most unlikely man, all in the same week.

That's why what she was about to tell him would be the hardest thing she'd ever had to do in her life.

# CHAPTER TEN

"TELL me what you need." Jared wrapped Kasey tight against his body, and she almost succumbed to feeling safe. "I'm here for you," he said.

"I don't want your pity." She pushed away from his chest, trying to roll away.

"I'm not pitying you, I'm consoling you." He wouldn't let her go. "That's what friends do."

She quit fighting him. He admitted he was her friend. That was something, but was it enough? And what about that look she'd glimpsed in his eyes when they'd made love? Truth was, she couldn't deal with her diagnosis and confused heart, and Jared offering his friendship when what she really wanted, if she was being honest, was so much more. Their simple, no-strings relationship was tainted now. She'd never know if he'd stuck around because he felt sorry for her or if he really cared. It was all too confusing. She had to put a stop to it. "Will you do anything I ask?"

"Yes."

"Then leave. Please. Leave and never come back or call."

As if the words had hit him like a sucker punch, it took a moment for him to answer. "You don't mean that." He tried to pull her close again, but she wouldn't let him.

"Yes, I do."

"Come on, you're just all shook up." He held her by the shoulders and tried to make eye contact. She didn't cooperate, afraid of what she might see, of being convinced too easily her plan was full of holes. "You're not thinking straight. You need me now more than ever."

"I don't want to need anyone. I hardly know you."

He gave her a gentle shake. She still refused to look into his eyes. "You know me better than any person in my life right now. And I think I can say the same of you."

"In the bedroom, Jared. Only in the bedroom." She tried not to watch his mouth tighten into a straight line of disapproval, tried not to think of how it would be to never see him again. "You're just someone I happened to know for a couple of weeks. Someone I screwed. That's pitiful. Isn't it?" Finally, she glanced at his eyes, saw the hurt and disbelief there, then flicked her gaze away because it hurt so much. Hit and run. She couldn't get sucked into emotion.

"Not from where I'm standing. I think what we've got is pretty damn great."

"Please go, Jared. Just go." She squirmed like a child in trouble, needing to do something drastic.

"I won't do it."

Houdini quick, she disengaged from his grasp, jumped out of bed, and hit him with her pillow. "Go!" she yelled, hitting him over and over again, letting all the pent-up frustration and anger at her circumstances take over. "Go away."

He crossed his arms to cover his face, ducking with

each pelt of the pillow. "You're being unreasonable. Hysterical." He rolled off the bed and stood. "Calm down."

She couldn't let him close again. "No! Go away. Leave me alone!" she said, ready to hit him with the pillow again. "I don't want you here."

He raised his hands in surrender, an odd, unidentifiable expression on his face. Defeat? "Is that what you really want?"

Steeling herself against whirling emotions and a deep pain in her sternum, she drew a calming breath. "Yes. Please leave."

The muscle at his jaw bunched as he pressed his mouth into a thin line of disbelief. His eyes probed with surgical precision, yet he didn't utter a sound. She didn't think she could bear another second of his scrutiny, wanting to take the pillow and cover her face. He must have sensed her desperation. He swallowed, bent to pick up his clothes, got dressed, and left without another word.

Once he'd cleared the house she dropped to her knees and let the tornado of feelings overcome her, tearing her apart, thrashing her against the walls until she surrendered. Sobbing, curled into the fetal position, she stayed on the wooden planks of her floor letting time slip by one heartbeat at a time.

She couldn't control the disease that toyed with her wellbeing, but she could control who and what came into and out of her life. Jared had found the key to a satisfying profession, he had two children he adored, and a future bright with possibilities. He was a California native and would move home as soon as his fellowship ended. There was no future for the two of them.

Did she even have a future?

The last thing he needed in his life was to be shackled to a wildcard like her.

Kasey had been the second woman in his life to kick him out. Jared slammed the car door and started the engine. His wife had done it because he'd quit caring. Kasey had just given him the boot because he *did* care. Would he ever figure women out? He shifted the car into gear but had the good sense to wait until he calmed down to pull into traffic.

He'd just made love to her in a way he'd never made love to his wife in thirteen years of marriage. He'd never wanted to please anyone more in his life. Since when had caring and consideration become a bad thing?

Well, to hell with her. He'd been kicked in the teeth enough and he'd had it. From now on it was all going to be about his kids and his profession. And getting back to California as soon as possible.

He pulled onto the road and immediately got honked at when he cut off a car. Not giving a damn, he cupped the crook of one elbow with his other hand and shoved his fist in the air when the other car swung wide around him. The guy gave a reciprocal gesture.

He'd had it with love.

Halfway down the street, the thought finally sank in. The word stopped him cold. Love?

He got another honk and remembered to put his foot back on the gas to enter the freeway.

Was that this crazy feeling he'd been carrying around with him lately, the odd sensation that nagged at him and kept him awake at night? The constant and unsettling feeling that there was so much more to take out of life, that he'd been squandering good solid feelings by shoving them deep down inside until they backed up and made him one miserable guy?

He shook his head. If this was love, who needed it? He changed lanes and got another horn toot for his efforts. What was up with his driving today?

Nowhere near ready to call what he was feeling for Kasey right this moment anything but being mad as hell, he stepped on the gas and headed for his exit.

Somehow Kasey managed to get through work. An onslaught of patients helped keep her mind focused on the job and not her troubles.

As she called in the ultrasound request for one of the regular Everett Clinic patients and waited on hold, she explained her reasoning.

"We've been putting this off long enough, Mrs. Driscoll. It's time to get an ultrasound of your gallbladder. You've been coming here complaining of dyspepsia for a couple of months, and last week we drew some blood. The lab results show an elevation of bilirubin, alkaline phosphatase, AST and ALT. These indicate something is going on beyond an upset stomach."

"What if it's gallstones?"

"First we see what the ultrasound shows. If there are gallstones, the radiologist will contact me and we can arrange for a surgeon to examine you. Oh, excuse me." The radiology department receptionist picked up the phone, abruptly ending Vivaldi's *Four Seasons* smack in the middle of the movement that sounded like rain. "Yes, this is the Everett Community Clinic and I need to schedule an ultrasound to rule out cholelithiasis." Kasey gave all the pertinent information then waited, once again put on hold, while the appointment date got worked out.

"These days, having your gallbladder removed is much easier," she said to the sixty-five-year-old woman. "They do it as day surgery, go through your navel, collapse the gallbladder, pull it out through a tiny opening, put in a few stitches, and send you home with a little drain in place."

"My goodness. That doesn't sound so bad."

"It really isn't. Of course, if there are complications, they'd remove the gallbladder the old way, and you might have to spend a day or two in the hospital."

"I'd rather have it the easy way," Mrs. Driscoll said, a pyramid of lines on her forehead.

Kasey smiled at her. "That would get my vote, too." The woman came back on the phone and gave the appointment date and time. "Great. Thank you."

Kasey jotted down the information, pulled one of her low-fat diet sheets from the file in the cabinet, and faced Mrs. Driscoll. "I've made an appointment at the radiology department for next week. Here's the date and time." Kasey handed the appointment sheet to her. "Notice there are instructions to follow down below there." She gestured towards the sheet of paper. "Stay on the low-fat diet from now on, and have nothing by mouth after midnight the night before the examination."

Kasey finished up with patient education, reassuring Mrs. Driscoll they'd take this process one step at a time. It made her think of her own circumstances, and how she'd have to take the rest of her life one step, one day at a time. After seeing her patient out the door, she quickly became distracted by her worries again, and wandered toward her desk.

Vincent must have sensed that something was up as he hung around the area, finding this and that to fiddle with. "Want to talk about anything?" he asked, avoiding eye contact.

"I'm fine."

He turned his head and stared. "You look like hell."

"Blame it on Arturo."

"Whatever, girlfriend." He brushed her off with a loose wave. "Yesterday you loved the cut."

"That was yesterday."

He shook his head. "When you're ready to talk, I'm all ears." He walked off in a huff, grabbing his laptop on his way.

Was her plan to alienate everyone she cared about? Dropping her head into her hands, she leaned her elbows on the desk, holding her breath and squinting to stave off the tears. It wouldn't work. Eventually she'd have to come up for air from fighting the steadily mounting sobs.


Jared made surgical rounds with the conjoined twins team on Friday afternoon. Amazingly, he'd managed a couple hours' nap after leaving Kasey's house, and almost felt human again. A team of neurologists was exiting the patient rooms when they arrived.

"Jared," Dick Ortega said. "I got that referral you sent me, and made an appointment for next week."

It didn't register. "Referral?

The neurologist must have read his blank stare. "The one for the nurse with Huntington's. I got your e-mail and expedited her appointment—plan to see her Monday afternoon."

"Hey, great. Thanks for that."

"It's the least I could do after the way you made my wife look fifteen years younger." The silver-haired doctor smiled with a knowing twinkle in his dark eyes.

Face lift? Tummy tuck? Oh, snap, both.

"What time's the appointment?"

"Four-thirty."

His surgical team had moved into Twin A's room, the girl named Estrella, so he thanked the good doctor. After all the headlines across the globe about their surgical success, her name couldn't be more appropriate. She was definitely a star. He rushed to catch up, not wanting to miss out on the first day's progress post-op, which gave all the signs of being phenomenal. Even with the historical ramifications of this surgery, the excitement of a dozen surgeons beating their chests with success, his mind had drifted somewhere else.

Surrounded by no less than thirty people, it occurred to Jared that Kasey had to face her future alone, and the thought sat like a boulder in his gut. He knew what it was like to be alone, how a person scarred up and lost the gift of feelings. She was too vibrant and full of life to allow herself to become one of the walking dead. Kasey had challenged him, debrided his thickened hide, and welcomed him back to life. Just like the cleft palate surgery had given him the clue that he wasn't content to be a cosmetic surgeon. She'd reached him through no-strings sex, sex that had turned into a surprisingly easygoing friendship, and much, much more.

Jared exited the hospital room along with his colleagues, smiling over the patient progress yet lost in his own thoughts. The "much, much, more" part of knowing Kasey was what worried him. How had it happened?

The answer didn't matter, because he was well beyond reason and logic. He was desperate. He'd hooked up with a nurse for some fun, had gotten in over his head, and had fallen in love instead. Didn't that beat all?

\* \* \*

All Kasey wanted to do was sleep through the weekend. She knew it was the coward's way out, but at the moment the wounds she bore were too tender for everyday life. She also knew she'd toughen up eventually, but right now she wanted to baby herself. Didn't she deserve it? She'd allow herself this one weekend to wallow in her cares, and then she'd do what she always did when life kicked her in the gut, she'd stand back up and get on with it.

On Saturday morning she hugged the pillow to her stomach and curled around it on the bed. *Stop thinking. Go back to sleep.*

Who the heck was knocking at her front door? She'd paid the rent. She'd also warned Vincent to leave her alone all weekend. He wouldn't dare stop by, unless he wanted to chance her wrath.

The doorbell rang. Three. Annoying. Times.

Kasey curled tighter, humming to drown out the sound, determined to let whoever the rude person was think she wasn't home.

It got quiet. Phew, they'd left.

New rapping came from what sounded like the back door. Was someone trying to break into her house?

*Don't get up. Ignore everything. The alarm is set. This is your weekend off.* Besides, it was probably Vincent being a PIA, even though she'd told him to leave her alone, and the last thing she needed today was a pain in the ass hanging around.

After another few seconds of silence, the damn front doorbell rang again. Could anyone on earth *be* this rude?

Tossing the pillow aside, she strode to the living room and looked out the peephole, soon needing to catch her breath.

Jared was at her front door, looking through the peephole back at her. All she could see was one huge blue eye.

"Go away."

"I want to talk to you."

"Our fling is over."

"Daddy, what's a fling?"

Kasey moved from the peephole and lifted a corner of the curtain. A spider-thin, preadolescent girl stood beside Jared. She wore straight-legged jeans and a fuzzy fake fur jacket with a hood, had wavy hair like her father, which was pulled back into a ponytail, and, well, she'd seen the girl's picture before. She had her father's eyes.

"It's what people who like each other do. We call it dating." Jared glared at her through the window. "Are you going to open up?"

It was his weekend to have his kids and, knowing Jared, he wouldn't miss it for the world. She noticed a healthy-looking boy on the sidewalk, playing Hacky Sack—the spitting image of his dad in baggy shorts and a bright red T-shirt. His dark brown hair was on the long side.

"You brought your kids here?"

"What else was I supposed to do? Desperate men do desperate things. Besides, this can't wait. Now open the door."

"Go away."

"You're going to turn me down in front of my kids? That's cold, lady."

"You're not fighting fair."

"I'm not fighting. I said I'm desperate. I want to make up with you. Now."

"Why do you want to make up, Daddy?"

Kasey grimaced. What was she supposed to do? Jared had brought the subject back up, and regardless of what went on between them the kids didn't need to be dragged into it. Why did he have to be so reckless?

"Because Kasey is my friend, and she's mad at me, and I don't want her to be." He said it so fast Kasey could hardly follow.

They hadn't had a fight. What she'd had was a rare moment of common sense regarding Jared. Could the little girl understand that?

"This is totally inappropriate. You shouldn't have brought your children here."

"Desperate times take drastic measures."

If desperate times meant that a man who only got to see his kids every other weekend might do something crazy like bring them along when he needed to make things right with her, he certainly had taken drastic measures. It was almost touching, but she couldn't let him sway her.

She opened the door a couple of inches. "I'm not dressed for company. Can you come back later?"

"I've made plans with my kids, and you're going to come along," he said, hands on hips, looking beyond manly. The word rakish came to mind. The tight polo shirt accentuating naturally developed deltoids, and narrow hips in snug jeans didn't help.

"I don't think she likes you, Daddy," the little one at his side said. Chloe. That's right. Kasey remembered her name.

"Trust me, she does. She's just playing hard to get."

"Am not!" How dared he make her out to be the stubborn one?

"Yes. You are."

"Hard to get?" Chloe repeated.

"She knows I like her. A lot. The same way Mommy likes Bradley, and she isn't making it easy for me."

"Is she your girlfriend?"

"Yes."

By now, Patrick had heard the ruckus, stopped playing Hacky Sack long enough to look up at the entertainment on the front porch. Chloe shrugged towards her brother, skipped down the steps to join in with Patrick's game. "Daddy's got a girlfriend!"

"As I recall, I was pretty easy to get," Kasey said in a strained whisper, once Chloe was out of earshot.

"That was before."

"Before what?"

"Before we got serious."

Was he serious? "When did we ever get serious?"

"Yesterday morning."

So he'd felt it too. Dear Lord, the man looked crestfallen standing on her porch, admitting he'd gotten serious with her, with his kids looking on. He really was desperate, and it drove his brows together as he stared at her with those dangerously blue eyes. This could be terrible for his ego, and mess up his kids for life. What was he thinking!

Desperate men often had poor judgement.

No one in her entire life had ever been despairing over her before. Desperate enough to drag their kids into the fray.

She was not going to give in and let him run roughshod over her just because he'd brought his kids as a lever. Cheap shot, if you asked her, regardless of whether or not he could find child care. She had no intention of letting the man, who was obviously out of his mind, get stuck with a health risk like her. She'd hold

him back in life, and she cared about him too much to
do that.

Oh, hell. She did care about him. Loved him. He
wasn't about to take no for an answer, even though it
was the best thing to do to just forget the whole damn
affair.

She glanced at the children by the curb, tossing the
Hacky Sack back and forth, then she looked back at
Jared, who had fire in his eyes, and an air of determina-
tion rolling off his skin. How would they work this out?

"Okay. You wait on the porch, because I've got to
put on some clothes," she said as she headed down the
hall hell-bent on not letting his little ploy change her
mind about the bigger picture. She'd be civil to him
and kind to his children, and patiently wait for the afternoon to be over.

Two hours later, they'd finished a trip around the Boston
Public Garden Lake on one of the pedaled swan-styled
boats. Both children had watched her closely the entire
ride. She wondered if she measured up. The children
had been shy at first in the car on the drive over, but
once they'd gotten to the park they'd opened up and
asked her questions as they'd walked. She'd done her
best to stay engaged with them, while being pulled by
Jared's audacious vibes. He had no intention of making things easy for her.

Once they got off the boat, the kids ran ahead to a
street vendor, looking for iced lemonade and a churro.
In an odd change of dreary May weather, the sun was
out and glistening off the water.

"I don't know what you have up your sleeve, but
I distinctly remember asking you to leave me alone."

"I did."

"For one day?"

"That's longer than I wanted to, believe me." He reached for her hand, but she moved away.

"Why?"

"Because I care about you. I don't want you to go through this mess alone."

She quit walking, and squared off in front of him. "For how long? How long will it be before you get tired of doing that? Before we realize we should have cut our losses a long time ago?"

"Friends shouldn't think like that."

"So are you saying we're not hot sex partners any more, but now we're just friends?"

He wore a pained expression, eyes and lips turning downward. "Don't be that way."

"I've got to think like that. I can't let myself fall for someone who plans to leave in another year. Where will I be then?"

He offered a dead stare. She'd heard about his apartment with the can't-wait-to-get-out-of-town feel and the rented furniture.

"Look," she said, "I'm not trying to be contrary, but we've got to be realistic. We signed on for a fling and wound up with all kinds of extra junk thrown in. We didn't see that in the package deal when we bought it, you know?"

"Do you give a damn about me?" he asked.

"What has that got to do with what I'm trying to explain?"

He took her hand. "Something changed between us yesterday morning. I know you felt it too. I can't walk away from that just because you tell me to."

She couldn't let him hijack her plan. The guy didn't deserve one more tether in his life. His kids looked up

to him and he'd just done something crazy on her behalf by dragging them along for the confrontation. He
was embarking on a new direction in reconstructive surgery, and he needed to be free of any constraints. She
wouldn't—wouldn't!—let him get involved with her.

No matter how much she wanted to.

With the kids busy buying treats from the vendor
three hundred feet away, she gave him a rueful smile.
Damn if her lower lip didn't tremble. "Look, I gotta go."
She couldn't let him see her tear up. "This isn't going to
work out. Let's face it now." Before it hurt even more
than it already did. She turned and rushed toward the
passing crowd.

"Kasey." He called her name, but she'd started with
a slow jog and stepped it up to a lope in the opposite
direction from his kids. She knew he wouldn't come
after her and leave them unattended. "I'm not giving
up!" he called out.

That's what she was afraid of. She ran as fast as she
could out of the park, toward the Chinatown T entrance,
away from Jared and all the hopes and dreams to which
she couldn't let herself fall prey.

On Monday afternoon, after Kasey had given the third
rabies vaccination to Janie, she clutched the paperwork
in her hand and left the clinic early for her four-thirty
appointment with the neurologist in Boston. Vincent
had volunteered to go with her, but she'd decided to
take this examination alone.

The high-rise medical office was typical of many
such buildings with cold tile floors that made foot-
steps echo off the granite walls. A chrome and mir-
rored elevator took her to the seventh floor. The hall
felt compact, claustrophobic even, and quiet, thanks

to thick brown carpet. The narrow corridor was lined with framed prints and posters by famous artists she recognized. Miro, Picasso, Modigliani. Rather than enjoying the art, she looked straight ahead to the office at the end of the hall, wondering what she'd find out today. Maybe, just maybe, Dr. Ortega would be the one to tell her not to worry. Maybe he'd laugh and say, *Oh, for crying out loud, you got yourself all worked up over this? It's nothing. Absolutely nothing.*

A girl could hope, couldn't she?

She swallowed and opened the door to the waiting room then stopped abruptly. Jared sat in a chrome and wine-colored leather chair, watching her. His piercing eyes were determined yet questioning when he looked up. The usual effervescent feeling she got in her chest whenever she saw him still happened, and it surprised her. She should be angry. What on earth was he doing there?

She'd asked him to leave her alone, had run away from him at the park. Why couldn't she get the point through to him? They didn't belong together. Ever. Regardless of her feelings for him.

She couldn't make a scene. Not here. What was he trying to do, out-stubborn her and force his way back into her life?

He jumped to his feet and rushed to take her hands. "Don't get upset. I just want to be here when you're done with your appointment. Then we'll talk about anything you'd like."

Right now the only thing she wanted to do was pound his chest with her fists. He was driving her crazy with this "being there" for her business. Couldn't he let her suffer in silence as she was used to doing?

She bit her tongue rather than tell him to leave. A

wiser part of her conscience stopped her from overre-
acting. "Okay," she said.

Jared didn't want to drive her crazy—he wanted to
offer her support. She'd humor him. Let him stay. But
there was no way she'd take him into the appointment.
This was her business. Hers and hers alone. And after-
wards she'd search for a rear exit.

After checking in with the receptionist, she sat in
a matching chair against the opposite wall. She'd let
him stay—did she have a choice?—but in the meantime she'd do her best to make him suffer. She covered
her mouth with her hand and stared at the plush coffee-
brown carpet in silence until the nurse opened the door
and invited her inside.

As she looked up, without meaning to, her eyes connected with Jared's. He nodded. She glanced away, refusing to admit it felt reassuring, and followed the nurse
through the door.

How different it felt to be the one in the gown with
the opening to the back, sitting on the exam table lined
with a tissue-paper-thin barrier, having her blood pressure taken. She waited with her bare feet dangling over
the edge of the table as she thumbed through a surprisingly recent design magazine from the wall rack.
Try as she may, her pulse quickened with every movement outside the door. What if she already showed signs
of Huntington's, had been compensating for physical
changes, and hadn't even known it?

After a couple of taps on the door, a silver haired
doctor entered and introduced himself. "I'm Dr. Ortega,
and you must be Ms. McGowan."

She nodded. "Call me Kasey."

His inviting smile helped her relax a tiny bit.

After going through her list, he glanced up. "We usually recommend having someone with you during this examination to help you remember what we've talked about."

"No, thank you. I'm a nurse practitioner. I'll remember what we talk about."

"Okay."

"Have you noticed any personality changes such as irritability, anger, depression or loss of interest?"

She'd certainly been irritable and angry lately, but that had been for a good reason. Depressed? Who wouldn't be? Yup, she'd lain around in bed all day on Sunday, tuning out the world. Oh, hell, it all seemed circumstantial. "Not really."

"Have you recently had difficulty making decisions, learning new information, answering questions?"

She shook her head. Except for making decisions, she seemed to be waffling back and forth where Jared was concerned. And she'd pay a thousand dollars to answer the big question occupying her heart today— just because she loved Jared, did that make it okay to mess up his life?

"Any problems with remembering important information?"

She shook her head in double time.

"Balance problems?"

She remembered feeling clumsier than usual lately. "Maybe."

"Anyone notice you making involuntary facial movements?"

She screwed up her face, definitely a voluntary movement, and shook her head again.

"Slurred speech?" *Only when I've had too much to drink.* "Or difficulty swallowing?" *Only when she had a huge lump in her throat when crying.*

"No." Her reply came out breathy.

"Let's begin with a neuro examination, then."

She'd given enough abbreviated neuro exams at the clinic to know the doctor was not only assessing her nerve function, motor system and reflexes with his thorough investigation but her mental status and speech as well.

The extensive test would take over half an hour, beginning with her head and ending with her toes. He had her smell things, distinguish between hot and cold, make faces at him, show her teeth, smile, frown, puff out her cheeks, raise her eyebrows, stick out her tongue, shrug, walk heel to toe.

He had her hop in place, first on one foot and then on the other, and she flexed and extended just about everything that could bend. He measured her muscle strength with various tasks of resistance, while standing and lying down. Then he moved on to the sensory system, using various items to test her reactions to pain, temperature, light touch, and vibration. Finally, using his rubber hammer, he tested all the usual reflexes she knew about from her own training, and several more she'd never have thought of, ending at the soles of her feet.

Once he'd finished the examination, after writing in a chart for what seemed like eternity, he glanced up. "You seem perfectly normal, but due to your family history and recent genetic tests, I'll order a CT scan and an MRI. This will give us a baseline for future reference. My nurse will call you with the appointment dates."

Kasey let out her breath, unaware she'd been holding it for the last few seconds. "Okay. Whatever you suggest."

After he left the room, she got dressed, thankful to know that nothing, so far, was abnormal. Kasey didn't expect that to change overnight either. She'd cleared the first hurdle, but would have to go for the CT and MRI to see what they showed, if anything. Dared she think things were looking up?

Once she was dressed she headed back to the hallway, searching for a back exit. No such luck. A tiny flutter of nerves winged through her center at the thought of seeing Jared again or, worse yet, that he wouldn't be there.

The only remaining test for today was the one sitting in the waiting room.

Jared.

# CHAPTER ELEVEN

KASEY stepped into the waiting room to find Jared sitting exactly where she'd left him. She let out her breath. Those big blues peered up at her from beneath tented brows. He couldn't feign the look of concern, and it made the butterfly flutters go double time in her stomach.

What was she supposed to do about Jared?

"How'd it go?" he asked.

"Fine. He says I'm fine."

His brows smoothed, relief washing away the tension in his eyes as he stood and reached for her. "Fantastic."

Kasey believed him. He was on her side. He'd proved it on Saturday, rashly doing whatever he needed to do to make her understand, even to the point of dragging his kids along, and he'd shown up here today in support without being asked. How much more proof did she need? He cared about her, and right now that meant more than anything else in the world.

She let him enfold her and draw her to his chest. Man, oh, man, she'd missed being held by Jared. His usual citrus-woodsy scent welcomed her, and even the scratchy tweed of his jacket felt fantastic against her cheek. She sighed, relaxing for the first time in days.

"Dr. Ortega wants me to get a CT scan and an MRI."

She felt him nod. His hands rubbed her back, soothing her even more. She could get used to this, but knew she shouldn't. If she let go of her resistance, he'd entice her back into bed, and she knew in Jared's case food hadn't been the only way into his heart. In fact, she'd never even cooked for him. What would happen if he found out she was a great cook…when she wanted to be. No, she shouldn't even go there with him.

Her mind spun with confusing thoughts about Jared—how she should keep him at arm's length, banish him from her world, from her heart. But he was here, and he made her feel safe, and maybe just one more day with him was okay, just for emotional support. Suddenly amidst all the jumbled ideas she wanted to prepare him dinner for being here today, for forgiving her stubbornness on Saturday. For refusing to let her push him away.

Only a good guy with nerves of steel would show up here and wait, and that gutsy guy deserved to be fed.

"Are you hungry?" she asked.

"Sure. Where do you want to go?"

"I thought I'd cook us something. Is that okay?"

He pulled back to look at her. "You cook?"

Showing the first sign of spunk in what seemed like ages, she cocked a brow. "You don't know what you've been missing."

His mouth twitched, his eyes dancing from concern to bring it on. "Oh, yes, I do." He lightly swatted then caressed her hip.

She'd meant it about her cooking, but he'd obviously taken it the wrong way. "Hey, I'm only offering dinner. Friend. Because you've been so annoyingly nice lately, in a desperate kind of way."

The mouth twitch stretched into a wide smile and,

coupled with his afternoon stubble, he looked far too appealing. "Whatever. I'm there."

"Then let's get going." She stepped out of his embrace and immediately missed his warmth.

As they drove home in Jared's car, he quizzed her about the examination. She opened up about it, even made light of some of the ridiculous poses she'd been in. "I felt like I was taking a sobriety test."

His deep, healthy laugh put a full smile on her face. Her expression may have been involuntary, but it sure had nothing to do with Huntington's.

She glanced across the car at him, his noble profile, the way his thick, dark hair curled on his collar. What the heck was she supposed to do about Jared?

Jared and Kasey walked the aisles of the supermarket together. He couldn't remember the last time he'd shopped for groceries with a woman. She wore black slacks with low-heeled boots, a bright green cowlneck sweater that made her eyes pop, and a dark gray blazer. The new haircut gave her a sophisticated air, but that bright-eyed stare she gave while picking over the zucchinis and yellow squash looked nothing short of playful.

"Chloe said she thought you were pretty," he said, pretending to examine a tomato.

"She did?" She slid him a sideways glance while her fingers tested more vegetables.

"Yup."

He followed her to the next stand. "And Patrick thought you were weird for running off like that."

Her head dropped back. She sighed. "I can see why he'd think that. What a lousy first impression to make on them, but you forced me into it."

"He thought you were pretty, too, by the way."

She tossed her head and snorted. "Get out of town."

He couldn't resist, so he kissed her cheek. "Not without you." She didn't push him away. Progress.

Kasey was a breath of fresh spring air after a long New England winter, and a welcome change in his life. He was definitely ready for a change.

After she chose a red bell pepper, she assigned him the job of choosing the crimini mushrooms, as she'd moved on to the fingerling potatoes. On the way to the butcher counter, he grabbed a bottle of white wine, a pinot grigio, as she picked out some chicken cutlets. His mouth was already watering and, watching her, the Pavlovian reaction wasn't all from food. She shopped with confidence, sure of what she wanted. If only she could feel the same about him.

It wouldn't be easy, but he was determined to convince her to give him a chance. He wouldn't be like the other men in her life.

Would he?

Back at her apartment, he was banished to the living room while she prepared dinner. The aroma emitting from the kitchen piqued his appetite. He nibbled a pretzel or two from the dish on the coffee table by the sofa, took an occasional drink of the not great but very drinkable wine, and scratched behind Miss Daisy's ears while watching the news on TV. From the loud purring, and insistence about his continuing on with the petting, he gathered the cat liked it.

He needed to come up with a plan to make Kasey purr tonight.

"Dinner's almost ready," she said. He sure hoped so because the combination of garlic, parmesan, olive oil, and pan-seared chicken was driving him crazy with hunger. So was she.

"At least let me set the table," he said, jumping up and disturbing Daisy, who'd settled in his lap. The cat protested with a protracted meow.

After Jared washed his hands and set the table, Kasey brought out the dinner on a single large platter. The chicken cutlets were lightly breaded and browned to perfection drizzled with a thickened lemon sauce and placed in a row down the middle. The sautéed veggies were on one side, and the golden brown buttered and herbed roasted fingerling potatoes lined the opposite side.

"I think I need to take a picture of this," he said, smiling.

"You going to post it on your social network page?"

He made a goofy face. "I might." Never occurred to him. He didn't even have a social network page.

As beautiful as the food looked, it tasted even better. "You've been holding out on me," he said, using the stabbed potato on his fork for emphasis. "This is delicious. And the chicken, wow, great, just great."

"There's so much you don't know about me," she said, teasing him with a flighty expression while sipping her wine.

She'd fed him an opening line, and he needed to take advantage of it. "I'd like to know everything about you," he said, feeling as earnest as all hell, wrists resting on the table as he leaned toward her.

She paused and gazed at him.

"I'm serious," he said.

"You'll be leaving next year, Jared. What's the point?"

He was well aware that she didn't need a lecture on taking it one day at a time and seeing where it led when she could very well be the one left behind. That had happened once too often to her, and though he couldn't predict what the future held for them, beyond what he wanted it to, nothing was certain in life. "So you can read the future? Are you a fortune teller?"

In mid-bite she stopped to give him an annoyed glance.

"I'm just saying," he continued, "we don't know what the future holds for us. All we can do is enjoy what we can of it."

"Is this the part where you try to talk me back into our no-strings fling?" She cut off a piece of chicken with extra vigor. The suspicious stare wounded him. He hadn't made any headway in the trust department with Kasey.

He should have waited until after dinner, because the conversation was affecting his sense of taste. Great dinner or not, he needed to get some things off his chest. Before she kicked him out of here tonight he needed to make sure Kasey knew where she stood with him. "No. This is the part where I tell you exactly how I feel."

He glimpsed an alarmed look in her eyes as she rapidly chewed her food. He refilled his wine glass and topped off hers, then took a long drink as he'd suddenly developed a deep thirst.

"We've done everything backwards, Kasey. We hopped right into bed without getting to know each other, discovered we really dug each other in there..." he pointed through the dining-room wall to where her bedroom was "...and we, I at least, realized how much I liked you. How I admire your dedication to your job and how you'd pulled yourself up by your own bootstraps and made something of yourself. Hell, I discovered that the first day I'd met you." He watched her pushing her food around her plate instead of eating, listening to every word. "At the coffee bar that night, when you'd let slip how you'd been handed a lousy diagnosis from a father you'd never even met, I knew you weren't any ordinary lady. Yet you still held your head high and refused to let it get you down. That was amazing." Their gazes met and fused. "You're amazing."

She quickly glanced away. He took another bite of food and drank more wine, waiting for his words to sink in. "The thing is, you're my game changer, Kasey."

Her head shot up, she nailed him with her stare. For someone who didn't usually hold back her thoughts, she'd gone eerily quiet. If he could only read her mind.

"Remember," he said, "you told me to be the game changer in my relationship with my ex-wife. You told me to fight for what I wanted with my kids." He pushed out his chair, stood, and walked behind her, resting his hands on her shoulders, then whispered, "You're my game changer. I didn't think I wanted another relationship for as long as I lived. Now I understand I'll never be truly alive if I don't have another relationship. And I want that relationship to be with you." He squeezed her shoulders, hoping she'd understand. "I want to be with you, Kasey. I want to find out what happens when you and I quit hiding behind our walls and instead start pulling them down brick by brick." He knelt beside her so he could look into her eyes, which were welling up. "I know what may happen with you, Kasey, and I'm dead serious about seeing you through it." Big, fat tears brimmed in her eyes and some dropped over the lids. "Give me the chance to prove myself, sweetheart. I love you."

Her fork clinked onto her plate. She shook with emotion. He thumbed her tears away and hugged her close, then kissed her hair.

"I do love you. Even though I don't totally know you yet, I already know enough about you to fall in love." He kissed her cheek. "You've got to believe me, because I'm not a liar."

Kasey let go a ferocious cry, flinging herself into his open embrace. He'd risked it all, and reaped an amazing result.

"I love you, too, Jared," she said, burying her face in his shoulder.

He'd finally heard the sweetest words on earth, and it made him feel as though he was floating in the air.

Kasey used the cloth napkin to wipe her face and eyes. Smiling, and refreshed from a long-overdue cry, she shook her head. "I must look frightening."

"You look beautiful."

Her knees turned to butter, seeing the sexiest man on earth with eyes only for her. Her fingers trembled as she gave one last swipe under her eyes.

Her body had just gone through the entire list of life's emotions and now a warm pooling between her legs added another. Lust. She wanted him. "What do you say we clear the table and have dessert in bed?" she said.

Every cell in her body was marked to want Jared. He looked longingly at her—so long and sexily she could count it as foreplay. Jared held out his hand, she took it, accepting the warmth and electricity of his touch, and together they walked to her bedroom.

The instant they passed the threshold he grabbed her shoulders, held her still and kissed her yielding lips. His tongue soon made love to hers as they held each other so tight she could already feel his arousal. Could anyone else's body ever feel as right next to hers as Jared's? He kissed her again. Easy answer. No.

She caressed his hips and pushed him tighter. Why

176 DR TALL, DARK...AND DANGEROUS?

did they have to have clothes on? Pulling away, she tried to unbutton his shirt, but he stopped her. His firm stare communicated without a doubt that he planned to take charge of this party.

She'd never surrendered completely to anyone, couldn't trust enough to let it all go, but this was Jared. The man had just told her he loved her, and she knew he'd meant it. There was something else she knew without a doubt. She loved him back.

With her breathing steadily mounting as he delicately removed her sweater and slacks, and with tingles and shivers rushing over her skin from the dome of her head to her nearly curling toes, she let him undress her garment by garment until she was naked and positioned on her bed.

Jared was fully clothed when he leaned over the bed and started applying butterfly kisses to every erogenous zone she possessed, beginning at her neck. Her breasts tightened and pebbled as his mouth found each one, teasing the nipple with his feathery tongue lashes. With each kiss and suckle, she gave in to him, riding the beautiful wave of excitement from a whole new perspective. She wanted to close her eyes to enjoy it more deeply, but didn't want to stop watching him. His kisses moved to her stomach, playfully nipping at her navel, making her squirm, before he continued south to her core.

The sweet torture went on until she twisted and writhed on the sheets, fisting them tightly, while he kissed her most sensitive spot as thoroughly as he'd kissed her mouth.

Not usually one to beg, she pleaded with him, called his name as if it was all she had left to hold onto now that he'd taken complete control of her body. Tension built steadily, the sensation so delectable she selfishly never wanted it to end. She indulged in the exquisite pleasure, her body coiling tighter and tighter, until she couldn't bear it any more. Jared took her to the tipping point with his loving tongue, and she dove into the releasing waves as they rolled from gentle to tsunami in strength.

"Now," she said, "I need you now."

Jared removed his clothes in lightning-quick time, and while she still rocked with the climax he'd given her he climbed onto the bed and thrust inside, immediately heightening the already amazing sensation. She wrapped her legs around his hips and he filled her, finally satisfying the missing link to her total satisfaction. He continued to take complete control as he held her hips tilted just so and they rocked together at his pace, a hard and driving tempo. The deeper touches awakened new points of awareness that heated up, spilled over, and traveled her body like rogue waves of pleasure. Her head frantically moved from side to side as he pushed her against the mattress time and time again.

Nothing had ever been like this, giving in completely to her man—the man who loved her. He worked her and drove her ever closer until the sublime moment where she felt him turn rod solid, throb, and with a wild groan spill inside her yet never let up on the piston pace. His massive climax swept her over the edge as she tightened in deep blissful spasms around him and let herself go to a place she'd never been before. Complete abandon. Completely at one with him. Completely his.

It was midnight before they ventured out for dessert. Famished from their nonstop lovemaking, they ate leftovers from dinner instead. Kasey had never felt happier in her life.

"So what happens now?" she asked, mouth full of chicken cutlet.

"You let yourself trust me as much outside the bedroom as you just did in there, and I promise I won't let you down."

She got up and nuzzled his shoulder. "I'm beginning to realize that."

"Then I'll just have to help you figure it out the rest of the way, too." He kissed her cheek, a greasy kiss from the potatoes. "What do you think about living together for a while before we make the big move?"

"What big move?"

"The one that takes vows and official papers and all that kind of thing."

"Hold on. This is moving way too fast for me."

"You're the one who just asked what's next. I'm only being honest with you. Like I promised. Remember?"

She shook her head. "You're blowing my mind."

"I thought I already did that in the bedroom. Let's see, about three times as I recall, give or take a whimper."

Kasey pummeled him with her palm, and he faked being hurt. "You're brutal when you're satisfied, you know that?"

"Are you kidding?" she said. "I can hardly lift my head."

They laughed and delicately danced away from the commitment conversation, and when they'd eaten their fill, they went back to bed. This time, since both had to be at work in the morning, to cuddle and sleep.

Kasey and Jared strolled into the Everett Community Clinic the next morning holding hands. Vincent shot up from his desk, his look of interest so obvious his mouth was open.

"Well, well," he said.

"That's only half of it," Kasey said.

Vincent's eyes bugged out and Jared laughed.

"Yes, we are," Jared said.

"Are what?" Vincent seemed to have trouble forming words.

"A couple," Jared said. "I finally convinced her about the shallowness of superficial sex."

Vincent clapped his hands, eyes sparkling. "Congratulations. And would you mind talking to my steady guy about that shallowness bit, too?" Vincent asked.

"Sure thing. Bring him to the bar on Friday when we celebrate. I'll clue him in."

Jared kissed Kasey lightly on the lips. "I'll be here tonight to pick you up."

"You will?" she asked, still amazed by the change in her circumstances.

He nodded and smiled as he backed toward the clinic exit. "And tomorrow night, and the night after that, and the night after that, and…"

# CHAPTER TWELVE

*Ten years later...*

JARED pushed Kasey in the wheelchair up the incline towards the car.

"What a beautiful graduation, Jared. Weren't you proud of Patrick?"

"Couldn't be prouder. Pre-med is a huge undertaking, but since he's interested in getting both an M.D. and a Ph.D. in research, that near free ride for medical school will help us out a lot."

"You would have been thrilled to pay every penny for him to go to med school, you know it." She smiled over her shoulder at him and he leaned forward so he could give her a quick kiss. "You need to let up on Chloe a little, though."

He shook his head. "She isn't even trying, Kase."

"By your assessment maybe, but not everyone is cut out for higher education."

"If she'd just applied herself a little more in high school, she could have gone to a four-year school instead of junior college."

"There's nothing wrong with junior college. That's how I started my nursing education."

"I'm not saying there's anything wrong with it, it's—"

"She's pursuing her interests, so get over it. Chloe needs to find out who she is, and that won't happen if you push her in a direction she doesn't want to go. You need to get it through your head that she wants to be a hairstylist and not a chemist."

Jared sighed. "Why do you always have to be the voice of reason?"

Kasey offered another bright-eyed smile. He still lived for those looks.

"One of us has to," she said.

He feigned shock. "If I'd listened to the voice of reason, I never would've ignored you asking me to leave you alone and not come back. I never would have asked you to marry me on the spur of the moment."

"And under different circumstances, I might have taken life for granted and decided you were like every other guy and blown you off, too."

"Sometimes bad things happen to great people, and good things come from it," he said, wheeling her over a particularly bumpy patch of parking-lot pavement.

"Going all philosophical on me, are you?"

"Just trying to put this Chloe business in perspective," he said.

"Give her time, darling. She's coming off a bad relationship. Her heart is broken. She's trying to stretch her wings and be independent. Give her time. That's what it took for you to get used to living in Boston, right? Time?"

"Time and the right lady. Heck, if a south shore girl like you could move to the north shore and get used to it, the least I could do was handle leaving the west coast for Bean Town."

He sighed, then spotted their car and rolled her to the handicapped spot for easy access.

"Before I met you," she said, "all I wanted to do was run my little clinic in Everett. If you'd told me back then that one day I'd be in charge of six community clinics, I would have laughed in your face. Hell, I could hardly handle one."

"You laughed in my face a lot back then, remember?"

"Only when you deserved it, dear."

When he bent over and reached down to put the brake on the wheelchair, Kasey grabbed his hand and squeezed. "If I hadn't been diagnosed with the Huntington's marker I might never have opened up to life or hung on for this wild ride with you. I've loved you fearlessly since you took the risk of telling me how you felt, and for asking me to marry you when you didn't have a clue what the future held for me, Jared. For us."

He hugged her and kissed her again. "And I'm incredibly grateful you took the gamble." He helped her stand. "Think of what we would have missed out on if you'd let pride win."

"I can't bear to think about it. I'd be a sad and lonely person who'd missed her chance of a lifetime." She hugged him with all her might. "And I would have missed watching Patrick and Chloe grow up, graduate from college. Well, one of them anyway. Didn't he look handsome today? Just like you did, I bet, at that age. Tall. Dark. Gorgeous. Some poor unsuspecting girl's worst nightmare." She looked wistfully at him. "Or dream."

He covered her mouth with a kiss, which, if he didn't put a stop to it soon, could get out of control for a parking lot. "And you would have missed all of Chloe's teenage angst," he said, after breaking off the kiss.

"How true. Maybe that part would have been okay to miss." She laughed and he joined her. "I love you so much."

"I love you, too."

He gazed into her eyes, now more beautiful than ever with a few creases around them from years well spent grabbing life by the horns and shaking it for all it was worth. With him.

Kasey hopped to stand alone while he removed the wheelchair. "How am I supposed to get everything ready for Patrick and our guests with this blasted cast on my foot?"

He opened the car door for her to slide in. "You'll manage, you always do. And I'll help."

"Why did you let me try snowboarding again?"

He bent and kissed her again. Smiled. "Because I've been married to you long enough to know that once you put your mind to something, there's no talking you out of it."

"Like loving you," she said. "There's been no talking me out of that either."

He stopped, love swelling in his chest, and grinned at the pride of his life—after his children, of course. "You know I love you, but promise me one thing."

"What's that?"

"You can sky dive, zip line, learn to ride a motorcycle if you insist, but from now on snowboarding is not negotiable."

"Yes, darling, whatever you say. You're the famous pediatric reconstructive surgeon."

"Since when has my professional title ever won me an argument with you?"

"Since right now, simply because you're taking such great care of me since I broke my ankle on our vacation. And since I've categorically decided that when I married you, nine years, seven months and twenty-five days ago, I officially became the luckiest woman in the world."

\* \* \* \* \*

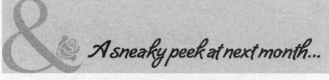

*A sneaky peek at next month...*

## Medical Romance™

**CAPTIVATING MEDICAL DRAMA—WITH HEART**

### My wish list for next month's titles...

In stores from 3rd August 2012:

☐ Sydney Harbour Hospital: Ava's Re-Awakening
   – Carol Marinelli

& How To Mend A Broken Heart – Amy Andrews

☐ Falling for Dr Fearless – Lucy Clark

& The Nurse He Shouldn't Notice – Susan Carlisle

☐ Every Boy's Dream Dad – Sue MacKay

& Return of the Rebel Surgeon – Connie Cox

**Available at WHSmith, Tesco, Asda, Eason, Amazon and Apple**

### Just can't wait?

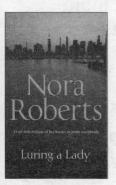

## The World of Mills & Boon®

There's a Mills & Boon® series that's perfect for you. We publish ten series and, with new titles every month, you never have to wait long for your favourite to come along.

---

### Blaze®
*Scorching hot, sexy reads*
4 new stories every month

### By Request
*Relive the romance with the best of the best*
9 new stories every month

### Cherish™
*Romance to melt the heart every time*
12 new stories every month

### Desire™
*Passionate and dramatic love stories*
8 new stories every month

# *Have Your Say*

## *You've just finished your book. So what did you think?*

We'd love to hear your thoughts on our 'Have your say' online panel
**www.millsandboon.co.uk/haveyoursay**

- Easy to use
- Short questionnaire
- Chance to win Mills & Boon® goodies

*Visit us Online*

Tell us what you thought of this book now at
**www.millsandboon.co.uk/haveyoursay**

YOUR_SAY